TANGLING SERIES BOOKS 1-4

PINEVILLE WORLD

DEBRA ELISE ROMANCE COLLECTIONS

DEBRA ELISE

Copyright © 2022 Debra Elise

Cover: Dragonfly Media Ink

Editing: Dragonfly Editing

All rights reserved. No part of this publication may be reproduced, distributed, or transmitted in any form or by any means without prior written permission. This book is your personal copy. This Book may not be sold to other people. Please contact the author at the email address listed below to obtain permission to excerpt portions of the text.

Publisher's Note: This is a work of fiction. Names, characters, places, and incidents are a product of the author's imagination. Locales and public names are sometimes used for atmospheric purposes. Any resemblance to actual people, living or dead, or to businesses, companies, events, institutions, or locales is completely coincidental.

TANGLING WITH MY EX / Debra Elise – 1st ed.

TANGLING WITH THE BREWMASTER / Debra Elise – 2nd ed.

TANGLING WITH THE COWBOY / Debra Elise—1st ed.

WORTH THE WAIT / Debra Elise—1st ed.

TANGLING WITH THE PLAYER / Debra Elise – 1st ed.

TANGLING WITH MY EX

Toni

I asked him to leave so he could heal, to find out what would make him whole again.

Gage

A former marine with attitude, PTSD, and dark fantasies Toni wasn't sure she could be a part of.

Now our daughter is getting married.

We haven't seen each other in four years. A weekend together, pretending to get along for the sake of our family, testing my sanity and my newfound desires.

I've dreamt about the things Gage described. Could I do what he wants, what he needs?

Maybe it's what I needed all along, too.

CHAPTER ONE

TONI

I ARRIVED AT THE RESORT WITH A SUITCASE FULL OF lingerie, a few toys, and two sets of wardrobes. One for the mother of the bride that I was, and the other to seduce and win back the man of my dreams.

Four years ago, my ex had given me the divorce I wanted. No argument. No fights. He walked away because I asked him to. Because he needed to heal from years of trauma witnessed in the military. I couldn't help a man who wouldn't help himself; it broke my heart. And he wanted more in the bedroom than I could give.

We were high school sweethearts. I got pregnant at seventeen, and we married soon after. He shipped out for boot camp less than a month after Lauren had been born. Gage was an awesome father, and I really thought we'd make it, even though he was on deployment more than home.

He'd finally left the service and made it home in time

for our daughter's sweet sixteen party, but he'd come home angry. Broken and quiet. The tough marine had refused to go to therapy. For himself. For us.

Instead, he wanted to tie me up and submit to him in bed. I couldn't. I was still the shy virgin girl he'd married fifteen years before. He'd been my only lover. And I'd been nothing but vanilla in bed. Maybe because of the long deployments and working and raising our daughter mainly on my own, had suppressed that side of me; I never explored my own sexual needs and desires. We never really explored or grown together in the bedroom. And then he'd be gone again, thousands of miles away.

He'd explained that his need to remain faithful to me had led him to watching videos to meet his sexual needs. Videos that had provided him with the physical release he needed and later craved.

But he'd become addicted to the kink he watched and wanted those same things from me. The things the women in the videos wanted; sex in public, to be blindfolded and dominated.

I couldn't do those things. I'd never been...confident in my sexuality. Always thinking my pleasure was secondary to my husband's. And also because you don't know what you don't know.

The last four years had provided plenty of time to think, and since I wasn't interested in dating, I turned to reading. And what I read excited me, turned me on, and made me miss and think of Gage. His body had been honed to muscled perfection during his years as a marine, so whenever I fantasized about the steamy romances I'd become addicted to, it was him, always him turning me on and fulfilling my every desire.

And then I stepped way out of my comfort zone and

found someone to teach me; no strings, no worry about emotions getting in the way. I went to a club and found a Dom who was willing to help me explore my turn-ons and desires.

Our daughter's destination wedding in Mexico became the perfect opportunity to seduce my ex. I just hope it's not too late.

Doubts had plagued me on the flight. What if he brings a date? What if he doesn't bring a date but is no longer interested in me?

After I checked in, I calmed myself with a long bubble bath and a cool, crisp glass of chardonnay to further settle my nerves. The ceremony and rehearsal dinner was in two hours, and I would see Gage again for the first time in four long years. We'd spoken on the phone a couple times a year to discuss Lauren's grades or graduation, which he missed, and at least once a month for the last six months to talk about her wedding and our shared costs.

And after each of those phone calls, with his deep raspy baritone still ringing in my ears, I would spend the night with my vibrator thinking of him.

But I never told him. Told him I now wanted the things he'd once fantasized about doing to me. I never once asked him if he still wanted me.

But tonight, that would change.

While drying off from my bath and imagining all the places I wanted him to touch, the phone rang, and my hand shook as I picked it up. I'd asked the front desk to inform me when he checked in. With this call, I would learn if Gage had checked in alone or with a woman.

"Hello, Ms. Holden. This is the front desk. You'd requested a courtesy call to let you know that the father of the bride has checked in. He's on his way to his room now, ma'am," the cheerful voice said.

I took a deep breath and asked the toughest question of my life, "Was he alone, or...?"

A long pause greeted me. "Um, yes. Mr. Holden checked in alone, ma'am."

I let out an uncharacteristic, hysterical sounding laugh. I quickly recovered and took another deep breath. *Relax, Toni. This is what you'd prayed for.* "Thank you. You've been very helpful."

I finished primping and prepared myself for a night of long-awaited fulfillment. I smiled as I chose a crotchless set of panties and matching bra, lathered lotion over my smooth legs and thighs, and stepped into my above-the-knee, body-hugging red dress.

Looking at myself in the mirror, I allowed myself to feel proud and admire the woman I'd become. Curves in places I was now okay with. Gone was the too-thin teenager and young mother who thought starving herself equaled beauty.

I looked pretty damn good for thirty-seven. Finger combing my caramel highlighted dark brown hair, I fought back the butterflies. He'd always loved running his hands through my long locks, and after a rebellious and regretful blunt cut shortly after the divorce, I had kept it long ever since.

My body lit up at the thought of him wrapping a hand through my hair to hold me in place as he pounded into me from behind as I bent over a chair, or a desk, or maybe the railing on the balcony of my room. I had plenty of fantasies of my own I wanted to play out.

My phone alarm chimed six-fifty p.m., time to leave. It was now or never. My pussy clenched at the thought of him inside me again. I smoothed a hand over my stomach, settled my nerves with a deep breath, and did a slow countdown from ten. The anticipation of his reaction amped my confidence. I slid into my black heels, picked up my matching clutch, and left to meet up with the wedding party at the ceremony rehearsal and the man I planned on seducing.

CHAPTER TWO

GAGE

Damn.

Toni was stunning. She'd was always beautiful, but now...she took my breath away and I felt a familiar twinge, the beginning of an erection I needed to tamp down—somehow.

I'd spent the last few years trying to get her out of my system. Shit, I knew I couldn't dwell on the lost time because I'd dealt with my PTSD, something she'd begged me to do for a year before she'd given me my walking papers.

I didn't deserve a second chance, but I'd finally gotten my act together, and now, after a year of intense therapy, I was a healthier, mentally stronger version of the man she'd fallen in love with. And I gave back and now helped fellow veterans work on their mental health as well.

And now I was determined to win her back. I'd arrived ready to seduce my hot and gorgeous ex.

As we walked through the rehearsal with the pastor, we made small talk, and I fought hard to stay on my best behavior. I didn't stare too long or kept my touches light and brief. Because I might not want to let go. Her body had always turned me on; however, she'd added a few curves since I'd last seen her, and I couldn't wait to get my hands on them, on her.

I was at risk of embarrassing myself as I forced back the temptation to drag her off to a dark corner and relearn every inch of her.

Toni had been my ideal woman forever, but now she projected a confidence that was fucking sexy. And I'd make her mine again before the weekend was over.

With the rehearsal done, we all went to the resort's private dining room for dinner, and I let my gaze sweep down her body as I stood across the room, taking in every luscious inch of her.

She'd never dressed this daring when we were together. As my gaze took in her luscious form, I noticed Toni's nipples poking against the material of her dress, and I froze. Who was turning her on?

The tropical heat in the Cancun resort meant air conditioning was everywhere, but with the sliding doors to the top floor banquet room wide open and allowing the cook night air and ocean breeze in, the air conditioning wasn't on.

Toni's body was definitely reacting to someone. Had I missed something or someone? Had she brought a guy with her?

Shit. I hadn't thought about having competition. Lauren never once mentioned her mom was dating anyone.

I gritted my teeth and continued checking her out. My gaze landed on her beautiful face, and lust slammed into me —full force. She was staring back. And holy hell, it was me her body was reacting to. I looked to either side of her. Just to make sure. No guy anywhere near her as I continued to eat her up with a look I hope left no doubt what I was feeling.

My dick twitched as I saw interest flare in her eyes. One of her hands flittered up to her neck, and she toyed with the necklace nestled between her lush, full tits. A soft smile playing on her lips. I held back a groan as Toni tore her gaze from mine. Was she flirting with me?

The mother of the groom joined her, breaking the spell. I took the moment to absorb the possibility that maybe, just maybe, I could win her back.

Taking a sip of whiskey, I couldn't keep my eyes off her. Damn, her legs were driving me crazy. Her feet, encased in a pair of kitten pumps, ignited a fantasy of us together...no clothes and those pumps still on her dainty feet as they balanced on my shoulders as I pounded into her.

I wiped a hand over my face and looked away.

Get it together, Gage. You have two days to get her underneath you again. Shit, I'm on the verge of embarrassing myself at my daughter's wedding. I don't think it would thrill Lauren to see her father salivating all weekend over a woman, even if it was her mother.

Unable to keep my eyes off her, I noted Toni's honey-blonde hair was longer than I remembered. And that dress she wore was a hell of a lot tighter than anything she'd owned when we'd been together.

Hell, why had I let her talk me into a divorce?

Oh, yeah. That.

Well, I was over—okay, mostly over my need for kink in the bedroom. But I was definitely better in the head since I'd been seeing a therapist at the VA. And I'd found no one to replace her.

Yeah, I'd had my share of one-nighters over the years, but when I closed my eyes, they were all Toni.

And now here she was looking like my best wet dream—ever, and I couldn't do a damn thing about it until much later.

After cocktails had been served, I finally got a moment alone with my daughter.

"Hi, Dad. You look deep in thought. Everything okay?"

Lauren was the perfect combination of Toni and me. I was so proud of her when she'd graduated high school early and entered the nursing program at the local college. And even more proud that she'd overcome her parents' failed marriage and still believed in love.

I wanted to tell her that I never stopped loving her mother. But I needed to tell Toni first.

This weekend, hell tonight if I could swing it, I was going to show my sexy ex just how much I still loved her.

"Hey. Is your mom...is she—oh, hell. Is your mom seeing anyone?"

"Who, mom? Um, why?"

Ever protective of her mother, Lauren crossed her arms and stared me down, well up, since she barely reached my shoulder. There was no way I was going to tell my almost married daughter why I wanted to know her mother's relationship status. Or the things I wanted to do to her.

"Ced, you okay? What's up?"

"Nothing. It's just if she's not here with someone; then... well, I thought we could sit together at dinner."

His daughter was no dummy. The corner of her mouth lifted in a smirk identical to mine. She relaxed her arms and gave me a quick kiss on the cheek.

"She's alone. In fact, no boyfriends, as far as I know

since you, uh, left. I'm pretty sure she still loves you, you know."

That news shook me. I gave her a quick hug and stepped back as her fiancé approached.

"Sir. Dinner's about to be served. Mind if I reclaim my bride?"

I nodded at the man who'd won over my strong-willed daughter—just like her mother.

Reclaim. Man, I liked the sound of that. I planned on doing some reclaiming of my own just as soon as I could get Toni alone.

CHAPTER THREE

TONI

My nerves were shot. I was sitting with Connor's parents and Gage. We still hadn't had a moment alone, but oh, my, the way he looked at me earlier...like he wanted to throw me over his shoulders and march me up to bed. Or was that wishful thinking?

Dinner was almost over, and I'd taken innumerable glances at him. He looked sharp in a suit. I wasn't used to seeing him in anything but fatigues and gym clothes from when we'd been married. He had wide shoulders and muscled arms.

I missed running my hands over his toned chest and the ridges and angled grooves of his abdomen. He'd always been in shape, and now retired, he looked just as fit as when he'd served.

"So, Toni, Connor tells me you have an Etsy shop. That's so exciting. I love supporting local artists. What's the name of it?" I hesitated before giving the name of my shiny new adventure to Connor's mom. What if she hated my stuff? What if she only bought something out of pity?

"You started painting again? That's fantastic." Gage inched closer.

I felt my cheeks warm at his praise. I'd stopped painting when I went back to work after Lauren had started elementary school. There had been little time and funds to pursue the hobby I had once hoped would become my career.

I turned toward Gage and searched his handsome face. The years melted away, and the fact we'd only spoken on the phone up until today didn't matter anymore. He appeared genuinely interested. My art had been a source of resentment when he was home between deployments. He'd been selfish back then, wanting all my free time to be spent with him.

"Yes, I started back up a couple of years ago. Pretty slowly at first, painting just on the weekends. But it took off, and I'm doing commissions now as well. I'm hoping to go full time soon and quit the bank."

Unspoken words filled the space between us. Old wounds forgotten. His interest was real, and I sensed a need from him I hadn't in so very long. He was attempting to reconnect. The thrill of possibilities settled within me. After all that had happened between us, could tonight be a new beginning?

"I'm really proud of you, Toni. I know how much painting always meant to you. When we were married, I thought you were talented, even though I complained about it a lot. I'm happy for you."

His words filled me up. Made me wish he'd said them years ago, but I'll take them now. He seemed different from what I'd remembered. Lauren had told me he'd been going to the VA for therapy, and he'd started working as a security consultant after he retired, but...could he have changed enough for us to be together once more? Suddenly, my planned seduction took on a whole new level of desperation.

A desperation to show him I could now accept him as he is and what he desires. I wanted to be the woman to fulfill his needs.

"Hey, you okay? What's going on in that pretty little head of yours?"

Gage's concern warmed me to my toes. When he reached for my hand and curled it into his, he rubbed a thumb back and forth over my palm. A snap of electricity traveled straight to my clit, and I let out a small gasp. It was the first intimate touch we'd shared since long before our divorce. It made me greedy for more.

At that moment, Lauren and Connor stood and began speaking. They told everyone in the room how much it meant to have their closest friends and family members here with them.

As others stood and toasted, Gage kept my hand in his, now hidden under the table. He continued his attention to my now overly sensitized skin. My entire body was now one massive, erogenous zone.

The innocent contact stirred up a need in me he might not have intended. I could feel my breasts become heavy with a desire to be touched. My nipples hardened, and I imagined him sucking on them until I came. Determined to get that and more, I looked up and found him staring at me.

I recognized that look.

I've dreamed about that look.

I returned his look.

A bomb could have gone off, and I would have continued looking at him. His nostrils flared, his lips tightened, and then everyone in the room began laughing and cheering—our moment broken.

We stood with everyone else as the father of the groom, who I hadn't even noticed had left the table, was entertaining everyone with tales from his son's childhood.

I swear I heard Gage whisper, "fuck me," as the crowd egged the man on to tell more stories.

I smiled to myself. *Oh, no. Fuck me, Mr. Holden.*

Before I could talk myself out of it, I tugged on Gage's hand to bring his attention to me. I mouthed, "meet me at the elevators."

His eyebrows shot up. I nodded toward the exit, let go of his hand, stood and walked away before I chickened out. I sent a wave to our daughter, then I took a quick peek behind me to see if he was following.

Gage remained where I left him. His eyes now hooded and zeroed in on me. He flashed me a peace sign, which I took to mean I had two minutes until he'd meet up with me.

I couldn't wait.

CHAPTER FOUR

GAGE

What the hell just happened? Did my ex-wife just give me the high sign to follow her?

Hell, yes, she did. I flashed her two fingers. I'd leave in two minutes, giving her a head start and allowing for enough time between our departures to make it seem less... fuck that. I'm going after my woman.

I arrived at the elevators in less than the two minutes she was expecting, but she was nowhere to be found.

"Toni, baby. Where'd you go?"

"Gage?"

Her voice drifted to me out of nowhere. Ramping me up with need, and she was hiding?

"Gage. Back here."

I looked past the elevators to where her voice seemed to come from. I followed a curved wall and ran into a short palm tree that hid an alcove at the end of the hallway.

An alcove to nowhere. Except this one was hiding Toni.

She was tucked up against the wall with the hottest come and get me look I'd ever received.

"Hi."

I didn't answer. I stalked toward her and stopped just short of pressing my full length into her luscious body. "You lost?"

"No, I'm right where I want to be."

"And where's that, Toni?" I almost couldn't wait for her answer. My cock was begging to be released, and if we didn't get on the elevator now and pick one of our rooms, it was going to be unleashed right here, whether or not she was ready.

"I've missed you, Gage."

"Ah, hell, baby. Please don't tell me that's the only reason you brought me out here."

She shook her head, and her long tresses fell forward. A soft curl landed on her right breast, and I swallowed.

She crooked her finger, grabbed my tie, and tugged me a couple of inches closer. "I want you, Gage."

My sweet ex-wife had always been shy when it came to sex and all things naughty. I didn't think she'd want me to do her right here. Hell, until this exact moment and seeing the look on her face, I hadn't dared thought the signals she was sending me had anything to do with hooking up in the hallway, steps away from our daughter's rehearsal dinner.

Yet here we were. But I didn't want to spook her. Whatever she wanted; however, she wanted it. I was ready to oblige.

"Tell me what you want, baby."

She gave me a wicked smile as I held my breath.

"A lot of time has passed, and I've changed, and I know you have too, right?"

I couldn't speak, so I nodded and then groaned as Toni

wet her lips with the tip of her tongue. She was nervous, but she was determined. What she said next blew my mind.

"Well, I've decided, and if you still want me, that I'd like to do all those things you wanted from me. All those naughty things...and I want to start now."

I watched in stunned silence as she took her hands and began lifting her dress until it reached her mound, covered in a wispy scrap of lace. Her hips came forward ever so slightly. The panties were crotchless, and her sweet pussy glistened. She reached down and touched herself and spread her pink lips. I was mesmerized.

"Baby. I—" My god, was this fantasy real?

"Ssh. I want this. You. Please?"

She didn't have to ask me twice. "Hell, yes."

I whipped off my jacket and fell to my knees, grabbing her by the hips. I leaned forward and took my first taste of heaven in a very long time.

CHAPTER FIVE

TONI

"Touch me, Gage. Make me come, now."

I'd practiced those words for months. I didn't want to sound hesitant when I finally said them out loud for the first time, leaving no doubt in his mind exactly what I was asking.

His first swipe had me lifting myself up on my toes. The second made me moan his name.

"Gage. *Yes*."

His tongue was magic. He flicked my clit softly. I was expecting more, but the light touch was electric, and stars burst behind my eyes. "More, please." I moaned.

"Christ, you're so fucking hot, baby."

Gage increased his speed and fucked me with his tongue. Oh my God, why didn't I ask for this before? "Yes!"

He spread me open with his thumbs and sucked my clit until I thought I'd fall over. The orgasm built. I was so damn close. "*Ahhh*, yes. I love that," I panted.

He'd stolen my breath. I grabbed the back of his head and pressed him closer. I needed him closer.

He sucked my clit again, then pulled back, released my throbbing nub, and smiled up at me. "So demanding. And such a pretty little pussy, but we don't have to do this here. I'm not sure where you've been hiding this side of you. I'm just damn glad it's me you're choosing right now."

Letting out a frustrated moan, panted. "Gage, if you don't shut up and finish right now, I'll...."

His chuckle held a sharp edge.

"You'll what? Let me fuck you in public? Is that what this is about, Toni? You trying to prove something? Because I'm over that. What I demanded of you four years ago was wrong, and I should have never let you talk me into a divorce. I still want you, baby. But we don't have to do this here."

Still dazed from having his tongue and lips on me again, I shook my head, then leaned back and pounded it on the wall. I gulped in air and had a decision to make. I was confused and horny. Mostly horny, but I needed to not be confused.

"So you're telling me you don't need kink to get off? That fucking in public, where anyone could discover us, is no longer one of your biggest fantasies?"

Gage stood up and pressed his large body into mine, and I melted. He cupped my face with his hands and kissed me gently on the mouth. I wanted to cry; his touch was so gentle.

"Baby, I've changed too. Right now, what gets me off is anything you want. Full stop. No kink, no exhibitionism needed. In bed with the lights out works for me."

I took a deep breath to clear my head. There was so much baggage that should have been discussed before I seduced him, but too late now. And there was no way I was stopping, either. My pussy was still throbbing.

"Let's make a deal."

Gage sighed. "What's the deal?"

"You finish what you started. I come, then it's your turn. We'll go to one of our rooms, and you can fuck me however you want."

Gage's hot breath fanned my neck where he'd begun nibbling.

"Jesus, that mouth. So dirty I'm on the edge of spilling inside my fucking pants. Deal." He groaned and trailed kisses down the middle of my body until he reached my curls and dipped back between my folds, and took another long lick. He brushed the edge of my hole. A set of nerve endings I did not know I had in an area I thought I'd ever want explored lit me up. And…oh, my God.

My core fired and spasmed as the orgasm rocked through me. My toes curled, my legs shook. I grabbed the wall to keep from falling, but Gage kept me upright and dived deeper. I let out a deep moan when a second orgasm started building.

"*Jeeeezus*, Gage," I panted. "Why didn't you just get me drunk four years ago?" I grabbed both my breasts and pinched my nipples. The sweet pain drew out the pleasure as I rocked my hips back and forth, riding his tongue. Yeah, I was greedy.

A starburst flashed behind my closed eyes, and I let the moment play out. This would be forever burned in my memory, and I couldn't wait to return the incredible pleasure.

Gage placed soft kisses on my swollen flesh. My body shuddered, coming off the highest high I'd ever experienced. He gathered me in his ripped arms, placed a cheek on my stomach, and held me tight.

I felt cherished, loved, desired. Everything I wanted and wished I'd been open enough to go after four years ago. But I shook off the quick flash of guilt and treasured this moment.

"Toni, I'm so thankful for this gift." Gage stood and adjusted himself.

Letting out a satisfied sigh, I straightened his tie. "I should thank you. That was...beyond anything I thought possible, and I want more. I want to take you in my mouth and—"

"Toni, you're killing me here." He let out a low growl and fixed my dress. "Now that you've had a taste of public sex, I'm taking your sweet ass to my room. What I have planned for you is just for us."

He captured my lips and devoured my next breath. Our tongues tangled, his hands threaded into my hair, tipping my head back.

"Mom, Dad?"

Lauren's shocked voice broke the erotic spell, and Gage pulled back slowly, capturing my gaze, and held it as we both sucked in air.

"Busted," Gage whispered.

His wicked smile sent another wave of heat coursing through me.

Connor joined Lauren. "Hey, babe, what are you doing? Why did you..." His voice trailed off.

"Oh, my...Connor, my parents are hooking up at our wedding." Lauren's surprise filled the air.

I peeked around Gage's shoulder. "Hi, sweetie. Um, I know this is kinda a shock, but..." My words died as I felt Gage's chest rumble against mine. He was in no state to turn and address our daughter, so I did what any good mom would and shooed Lauren and Connor away.

"So, nothing to see here. I'm sure you're both tired after a long day of traveling and the excitement from, well, everything. I'll see you tomorrow. Right on time to help you get ready, okay? I promise I'll explain everything. I know this is a lot to take in, but your dad and I have some things to work out, but it's your wedding. We're not going to do anything to take this moment from you or embarrass you. Okay?"

Lauren's shock wore off, and her eyes welled with tears. She covered her mouth and let out a garbled shout.

"Are you kidding me? I've been dreaming that you two would get back together." She turned and grabbed Connor's hand. "Okay, we were never here. Love you both." Laughter echoed off the walls as they made their escape, stepping onto the elevator.

Gage let his forehead fall onto mine, and he rubbed my shoulders. "You handled that perfectly."

"Thanks. I think. I hadn't really thought about anyone finding us, let alone our daughter and almost son-in-law." A rush of embarrassment took over my previous satisfaction from receiving not one but two amazing orgasms.

Gage must have felt the shift in my mood because he kissed my temple and held me closer, if that was even possible.

"We're two consenting adults. Free to explore our sexuality. There's nothing to worry about, babe. Seeing her parents together obviously made Lauren happy. But right now, all I care about is your happiness, okay? Because this isn't over. Not by a long shot, Toni."

He kissed the corners of my mouth and licked the seam of my lips. I opened for him and let all of my love pour out. God, he could kiss, and this one held so many promises.

Our tongues tangled. Our bodies heating again. His cock pressed into me, and my nipples became hard points as I pressed my breasts into his rock-hard chest, looking for relief. "Take me to bed, Mr. Holden."

"Baby, I changed my mind. I'm gonna take you more places than a bed before the night is over."

He grabbed my hand and tugged me toward the elevator. "How about we start in here?"

The wicked glint in his hazel eyes had my pussy clenching again at the thought of him inside me. But first, I planned on going down on him. The image of taking him into my mouth and giving him the same pleasure created a flood of warmth between my legs. I squeezed my thighs in anticipation.

Now well after midnight, did I dare fulfill another one of my fantasies?

As soon as the elevator door closed, I pushed the correct button to keep us locked in, and more importantly, others locked out. I reached for his belt and smiled. Gage's answering grin was all the incentive I needed.

Dropping to my knees, I freed his cock and ran my hand over its velvety, hard length. My mouth watered at the anticipation of tasting him again. I'd never thought it possible, but the thought of pleasuring him created another rush of warmth between my thighs.

My clit throbbed as I took him in my mouth and played with him until he grabbed the back of my head. I went deeper, and he shouted my name. He reached down and cupped one of my breasts and pinched a nipple.

"Shit, I can't wait," Gage pulled out of my mouth and, in a move that made me dizzy, reached under me, turned me, and guided me onto my knees and hands. My pulse raced in anticipation of the position and of him finally filling me again with his thick cock.

Lifting my ass higher, I then spread my legs wider and felt a tug inside me, my body instinctively opening—preparing for him. I heard him draw in a deep breath and whisper my name.

"Gage, please." My whispered plea ringing in my ears. Apparently, my patience had disappeared, and it was all about getting him inside me. I wanted the pounding, the fucking his growls and moans promised me when I'd been sucking him off.

As the seconds ticked by, my desire reached a crazed level, and I wiggled and rocked my hips toward him. My reward was a firm smack on the ass. Shock lasted for a mere moment before a flood of warmth hit me as my outer lips and clit became engorged.

"Naughty girl." Gage rubbed the spot he slapped, then trailed a finger along my slit. "I was admiring the view. I need you to be patient for me; otherwise, I'm turning your tight ass red. Or maybe that's what you want?" He returned his hand back to my tender flesh. "Just say the word, baby."

I nodded and pushed back further. Instead of another sweet slap, he dragged his other hand along my pussy and tapped my clit.

Oh, my, yes! A full-body shudder overtook me.

It was torture.

It was bliss.

I wanted him to spank me, to drill me, and I wanted it now.

My head dipped. "*Yeees*, I want it all." I growled the words. Me, growling.

The second smack ignited a fire within me I didn't want extinguished. I felt the rise of yet another orgasm as I began rocking against him, seeking relief, begging to be filled. His fingers or his cock. It no longer mattered. I needed to come—now.

"*Gaaage.*"

The sound of foil ripping reached my ears, and I breathed deep as the tip of his cock teased my now drenched pussy. Finally.

"You're so fucking beautiful." He leaned over my back, his cock pressing into my ass. He dropped hot kisses on my neck and whispered in my ear, "I know you're ready for me baby, hold on because I can't go slow, so tell me now if you don't want me pounding into you with my big cock."

"Gage, I need you inside me. Now!"

He lined himself up and thrust into me. The pleasure pain as he went deep lifted me high, and I spread myself wider and took the promised pounding. Our gasps and moans mingled as he filled me. Nerve endings ignited as I sobbed at the exquisite pleasure.

"Baby, you are so tight. I...dammit, I'm coming."

He reached down and worked my clit, sending me over the cliff as he stiffened and spilled hot and deep within me. His wicked fingers continued to play on my tight bud, prolonging the orgasm coursing through me.

The power of it had me sobbing his name over and over. Our bodies still fused—the sensation taking me to the brink of passing out—if only I'd known four years ago this was possible between us.

We curled around each other on the floor of the elevator, our breathing eventually evened out as our hands ran over each other. I trailed my fingertips along his still well-defined abs, up to his pecs and over his corded neck and shoulders. This was the most perfect moment of my life. And I wanted more. More of him.

"So...." Gage's voice hitched. Clearing his throat, he began again. "So, does this mean you're going to give me, us, a second chance?"

I looked up into his handsome and well-satisfied face and answered honestly. "No."

Gage's face fell. "Hell, isn't that why you seduced me?"

I tried to keep a straight face, but seeing his confusion and underlying hurt had me pushing him onto his back and climbing on top of him, sliding myself over his him as his cock perked up at the contact. Memories of his stamina when we'd been married slammed into me. A spasm squeezed my pussy in anticipation.

Once upon a time, I would beg off a second round, claiming I needed sleep. That was the old me. Today, I would take every last drop he had.

The inward thrill of owning my sexual needs ramped me up for more. I rocked against him, thrilling at his response.

"No, I seduced you to give *me* a second chance. I think we needed time away from each other to find ourselves and come back together, stronger." I held his gaze, and my heart burst at the love and desire Gage's eyes emitted. Proof it was never too late to start over. And oh, what a start.

"I love you, Gage."

"Baby, I never stopped loving you."

He lifted his hips, took his cock in hand, and impaled me. Filling me and stretching me on the floor of an elevator. I rode him till I was out of breath. I rode him till I came crying out his name.

EPILOGUE

One year later

TONI

Standing in front of the hotel's full-length mirror, I marveled at all that had happened since our daughter got married—since I took a chance on myself and Gage. Great sex, true love and reuniting our growing family, all of it fuller and better than ever.

There'd been so many lonely years that I now counted each day as a blessing that my husband, soon to be husband again, had gifted me with a second chance at our love and our new sexy times. Smiling at my reflection, I remembered all the ways we loved each other since the day I took the step I once thought impossible.

"Mom, you look beautiful. Dad is going to cry. I just know it." Lauren sniffed.

Turning at my daughter's words, I did that thing where

you laugh and cry at the same time. Pregnant with our first grandchild, she glowed and if I didn't stop looking at her, another round of crying was imminent.

"Thank you, sweetie. You feeling okay this morning?" She was in her sixth month but was still battling morning sickness. Probably because she was carrying twins. Opening my arms, she stepped forward so I could fold her into a tight embrace, filled with awe that my baby girl was going to be a mother soon. I couldn't wait to be a grandma.

It was almost time to go down to the beach, the very same one Lauren and Connor had stood upon almost a year ago, pledging their love.

Gage insisted we come back to where we reconnected to exchange our vows, but I think it had more to do with the little used elevator off the ballroom that had him eager to recreate one of the best moments we'd ever experienced together.

"Let's go. I'm sure your dad is already down there."

Lauren pulled back, then rubbed her belly. "He is. Connor texted me before I came in to let me know he's pacing up and down the beach, kicking sand everywhere."

Grinning, I suspected I knew why. I'd insisted we have two rooms when we arrived yesterday, well, at least for last night. I'd wanted to build the anticipation we'd both felt the first time we married and knowing Gage, if we'd been in the same bed this morning, we'd be late for our own wedding.

Sunrise was breaking as I stepped onto the warm sand with Lauren on my arm. The first thing I saw after taking a deep breath and lifting my gaze to the water's edge was the man of my dreams. I practically floated toward him. Tears filled Gage's eyes, and my heart swelled at the sight. I reached out to take his hand, and he pulled me into him, capturing my lips in a deep kiss that left me breathless. My body electrified and needy, I wrapped my arms around his neck, then whispered in his ear, "I need you too, but not in front of our family. I promise the minute we can go to our room; I'll race you there."

Gage threw his head back and laughed, the sound sending a fresh batch of tingles in all my, and his, favorite places. Reluctantly, he released me, then stepped back and the minister began the ceremony.

I'd never been happier than tangling with my ex, my groom—again, my everything—now and forever.

TANGLING WITH THE BREWMASTER

Twenty years is a long wait for a hook-up.
Laci Monroe

We attended the same college. I was his tutor, he was big man on campus, and I wanted him to be my first.

I thought the hook-up was going to finally happen at a frat party, but after an ex causes a scene—his, and too many shots consumed—me, I ended up giving his roommate that honor. A month later, I peed on a stick. It sealed my fate. Epic sad story.

Till now.

Luke Hart is back in town.

It's up to me to make the first move.

I just need to make sure he knows I want more from him than his prize-winning hard...seltzer.

Tangling with the brewmaster could be my best birthday present ever or another epic fail.

CHAPTER ONE

LACI

The first and third Fridays of every month was girls' night. Each week we chose a new place to blow off some steam, discuss our kids, and complain lovingly about our husbands, well ex-husband, for me. And believe me, it was never a loving complaint.

It wasn't typical of us to pick the same place twice in a row, but that was before Hart's Pass Brewery & Pub opened. Tonight was our second visit. And the reasons were pretty straightforward. Great drinks and the sexy owner and brewmaster, Luke Hart.

"Laci, you going with the Candy Cane hard seltzer again? I can't believe they're keeping it year round now. Oh, and look, they have Key Lime Pie hard seltzer mini cupcakes. Let's skip the sliders and have dessert instead?" Audrey, my closest friend in the group, grabbed my arm. She put her menu down, daring the rest of us to deny her request.

"Audrey, don't tempt me. We're not going to rehash this

old argument again, okay? Dessert is meant to be served and enjoyed after a meal." Blayne picked up Audrey's menu and handed it back to her. "I'll treat everyone to the cupcakes later. I need protein first. Otherwise, someone is going to have to drive me home after just one beer."

"Lightweight!"

"Deidre, hush. Now, everyone decide on which beer you want, and I'll flag down the server.

I'm ready for a drink after the day I had." Audrey winked at Laci. "Or maybe I should request

Luke come take our order."

I let out a sigh and shook my head. Audrey was the only one who knew about my long-ago connection to Luke. "I'm sure he has better things to do than entertain a table full of women who'll be going home to husbands who have no idea that their wives have been lusting after the newest pub owner in town."

Although I wasn't a beer lover, it was the area's first brewery to produce and serve hard

seltzer, which I preferred.

However, it had quickly become bittersweet torture.

And Luke Hart was the source of that torture. We were once friends. Classmates at the local university almost twenty years ago.

A lifetime.

During my sophomore, his senior year, I was his tutor. He was the football star who needed help with biology. And I wanted him to be my first. I thought the hook-up would happen at a frat party—finally, but after an ex caused a scene—his, and too many shots consumed; me, I ended up giving his roommate that honor.

A month later, I peed on a stick. It sealed my fate. Epic sad story.

The shotgun wedding two months after that long-ago night haunted me each time I looked

Luke's way. The whole *"what could have been"* had buried all those years but had now come

roaring back. And I had it bad for him. Probably more so now.

There were nights in my marriage where I closed my eyes and pretended my husband, Kevin, was Luke. At the time I felt guilty, but as the years passed and our sex life became non-existent, the guilt was replaced with detailed fantasies, and most of them starred Luke.

On our first visit to the pub, I'd thrilled at his expression when he'd looked at me, recognition dawning in his eyes as they'd widen, then his gaze darkened a bit, and I was propelled back in time and to our first tutoring session. I'd been instantly smitten, or more accurately in lust, but he'd showed no interest. So I spent a semester pining for him until that fateful last night. And now fate had intervened, and I was no longer the shy virgin. I spent that night trying to get my nerve up to approach him.

The pub was packed, and we never got beyond a few fleeting glances as one group after another commanded his attention. So, tonight I came armed with a plan and plenty of nerve. I excused myself from the group to say hello without the prying eyes of my friends.

I became more emboldened with each step I took as he watched me as I made my way to the bar. Unfortunately, he was holding court over a group of rowdy middle-aged men working their way through a tasting of the pub's darker brews.

I changed direction and visited the ladies' room. While washing my hands, I studied my flushed face from the hard seltzer and the emotional buildup of speaking to

Luke. I ran cold water over my wrists, hoping to cool down.

I needed a new plan.

On my way back, he turned and winked at me, his intense gaze following me as I kept him in my peripheral vision. So hot and bothered by the short interaction, I drained my glass of ice water as soon as I sat back down and spent the next hour avoiding the bar. So turned on, I feared if I did, I'd do something out of character and march over and proposition him in front of the group of men without batting an eye.

Our server appeared and deposited a fresh drink in front of each of us. "Compliments of Luke. Enjoy."

Audrey, Blayne, and Deidre lifted their glasses in gratitude toward the bar while I took a small sip before turning toward Luke. He flashed a smile and nodded to the table. But our gazes held much longer as my friends resumed their conversation. I half stood when yet another group snagged his attention, and the moment was gone, but not the anticipation of what could happen next. It was going to be a long night.

CHAPTER TWO

LUKE

I haven't been this frustrated since college. And today, as well as then, the object of my desire was Laci Monroe. The quick success of the pub had caught me by surprise. I'd been sure this area of the city was the perfect location for the brewery and pub, but the buzz was better than expected. I know I shouldn't complain, but the demand on my time was keeping me from her.

I'd heard she got divorced a couple years ago and knew she'd never left Pineville, but I hadn't expected the girl that got away to walk into my pub and make me wish I was twenty again.

Tonight I couldn't take my eyes off her. She'd filled out in all the best places a woman could. She'd been off-limits to me back then, and our tutoring sessions had driven me crazy. But the good thing about now was I'm free to do and see whomever I wanted. And I wanted Laci. It was instant lust all over again, and this time there'd be no one in our way.

Our shared glances were a good sign and led me to believe she might want the same. But every time I thought I could take a moment for myself, another patron wanted my attention, or a fan of my football days wanted a story.

I'd just about reached my limit in keeping the customers happy. If one more chance to talk to Laci passed me by before she and her friends left, my employees were going to see a side of me better left hidden.

"Luke, table six says he went to school with you and wants to know if you could stop and see him." The server took off to take another order before I could ask her to go back to table six with free drinks and an apology.

Dammit. I stepped back into a corner of the room and rolled my head and shoulders, working out the kinks from hours of standing. It'd been a month since the grand opening, and I still couldn't get used to being on my feet eight-plus hours non-stop in the pub on top of the hours in the brewery. My admiration for anyone who had a job where they were constantly on their feet had increased tenfold, but it had me dreaming of when I could step back from being the face of the business and concentrate fully on the brewing.

The eighteen-hour days were killing me. Really, I only had myself to blame since I decided not to take on a partner or hire a general manager so I could focus solely on the brewing. Shit, I needed a break. And the more I watched Laci, the more I wanted to take it with her. Over her, under her, and deep inside her.

"Uh, boss. You okay?"

Clay, my lead bartender, handed me a towel.

Looking down at my hand, I swore. I'd been filling a growler, or rather overfilling one, as I fantasized about Laci.

"Yeah, sorry, this one got away from me. I'm going to

take five and check the tanks in the back." Ignoring several shouts from my waitstaff, I left the pub's noise behind and went into the brewery. I'd decided to attach it via a long-covered hallway to the pub, knowing the winters could be brutal. I didn't want anyone injuring themselves trekking back and forth.

Stepping into the main brew room filled me with a sense of pride every time. I don't think it'll ever get old. I'd taken my biology degree that Laci had helped me achieve, and I worked my ass off and used it as my foundation when the microbrewing bug bit hard during my first offseason with the NFL and after I became injured and had to leave the sport I loved. Walking between the gleaming equipment, I couldn't help but make the connection between where I was

today and the help Laci gave me.

Her enthusiasm for education had bled over to me, and I turned my almost failing grade in biology to a solid B. It had meant not repeating my last semester of college. She hadn't known at the time how important the degree I'd earned meant to my parents and me. She never finished college that I was aware of after she left to get married to my jerk roommate Kevin. Man, I hadn't seen that coming. I knew Kev was hot for her, constantly pestering me to introduce them, but their romance, or whatever, happened so fast, and then she was pregnant, and I'd lost my chance.

Determined to find out if she was open to going out with me, I needed to figure out a way to find some time to talk to her. I couldn't seem to get Laci out of my head since the moment she walked back into my life.

My cell buzzed, and I let out a curse. "What's up, John?" I waited for my assistant to respond, then looked at my watch. Yeah, another day got away from me. Every sane person I knew had finished for the day, and here I was, still working. I gave the closest steel cooker a tap and let out a heavy sigh. This is what I wanted. Complaining about the hours was stupid. Others would kill to be in my shoes, given the initial success I'd achieved. Suppose they only knew the time it had taken to get here—going back to school for a second degree. In that case, this one in microbiology, traveling to Munich, and completing the master brewer program, plus the hit my personal life took.

But it was all worth it, even with forty staring me in the face. Hell, I was ready for more than the occasional hook-up.

"Hey, Boss. That distributor from southern Idaho is here and—"

"Yeah, yeah. Tell him I'm on my way." I flipped the lights off behind me. Once I handled this last request, I would approach Laci and at least get her number before she disappeared on me again.

When I walked back into the pub, my eyes roamed the crowd till I found the table where Laci and her friends had been sitting. A new group was now seated in their place. Shit, it was going to be a fucking long two weeks if she came back in at the same interval as her group's previous visits.

LACI

THIRD TIME'S THE CHARM RIGHT? THE LAST TWO weeks had crawled by, and I'd toyed with seeing Luke on my own, but something always kept me away. And frankly,

I let it. I guess I wasn't as confident where he was concerned as I thought I was. Today was the first Friday of the month, finally, and everyone agreed we should go back to Hart's Pass.

My cell buzzed. It was Audrey making sure I was on my way. Smiling, I took one last look in the mirror. I'd spent more time fixing my hair and agonizing over my outfit than usual, finally settling on a short but not too short skirt and a button-down, floral sleeveless top. I left one more button undone than I would have if I'd been going anywhere else but to go flirt with a man I've wanted for twenty years.

Fighting a rush of butterflies, I looked in my rearview mirror and added a swipe of lip gloss and left to meet up for girls' night. I thought about the conversation Audrey and I had at lunch earlier in the week, where I confessed my growing obsession with Luke. She listened; well, she didn't interrupt me, but the half-smirk she wore conveyed an "I knew it" look, and I giggled at the memory.

When I'd finished, Audrey went serious on me and grabbed my hands as I shredded a napkin as I told her how just being in the same room with Luke again had stirred up not so dormant feelings. Naughty and so unlike me, feelings of desire for a man who'd never kissed me, not once all those years ago.

"You deserve to go after him. Heck, the only good thing that came out of being with Kevin all those years were your girls, Jennifer and Emma. And now that they're on their own paths, you should take this time and explore those feelings."

And those feelings included an awakening, and an increased need for pleasure. Sex had been nice at best and sporadic and unfulfilling at its worst with my ex. And I found myself reading romance novels and marveling at the confidence the heroines had in their sexuality and asking their partners for exactly what they wanted. So, what if I've put on a few pounds since he last saw me? I felt secure enough that if my curves were an issue for any guy, then that guy wasn't for me. Besides, I'd had plenty of guys hit on me in the past two years since my divorce, so I knew I was still attractive and knew men liked a curvy girl, well woman.

But no one had lit me up the way Luke did when I walked into his pub last month. I had spent so much time the last couple of years getting my daughters through their final years in high school that I hadn't dated at all and had forgotten about that quick rush of desire that always hit when you saw a guy you wanted.

I felt lighter after sharing how I felt with Audrey, and she was right. I was still youngish. There was still a lot of life left to enjoy. Not that I wanted to get married again, but exploring new interests and what I wanted from my relationships was going to be my new priority. So, I was taking this chance to spread my wings. And I wanted to do that with Luke Hart.

We walked into the pub and headed straight to where Blayne and Deidre had snagged a table. Looking around, it was just as busy as last time, if not more so. Immediately, my gaze traveled toward the bar where I knew he'd be—drawing beer and entertaining everyone around him.

Lord, he looked better now than he did twenty years ago. His dark brown, slicked-back hair begged to be tousled. His rugged good looks and toned and muscular body belied the fact that he was forty now. The only thing giving his age away was a touch of gray at the temples, which only made him sexier.

I had so many questions I wanted to ask him. Why'd he come back to Pineville? Why a brewery? I'd racked my brain trying to remember if he'd ever mentioned his interest in brewing in college, but I couldn't. And it was apparent he loved what he did. He was a hands-on owner. And yes, I wanted his hands on me. My girl parts tingled, and my panties become damp at just the thought of us together.

I took another quick look in his direction after the server delivered our ice water, so everyone had more time to decide what they wanted. Tonight he wore a dark gray Henley, with the pub's logo stretched tight over his wide chest and broad shoulders. He was at the far end of the bar where a group of college-aged customers listened avidly to something he was saying. He commanded attention wherever he was in the room. Female attention. And he certainly had mine.

As if he knew I was watching him, his gaze zeroed in on me. He kept talking as we locked eyes. So much was conveyed in that unspoken moment I didn't hear Audrey saying my name until she bumped me on the arm.

"You need to go over there, Laci," Audrey whispered low so only I could hear her.

Her words snapped the connection I had with Luke, and he flashed me a quick smile before turning his attention back to his customers.

"Does he ever *not* look fine?" Deidre asked no one in particular.

"He must lift weights. His arms should have their own Instagram account. Damn. I need to get my guy to work out more." Blayne added.

I silently agreed with the first comment and chuckled over Blayne's as I finally picked up my menu and took a moment to settle my hormones. During our last outing, the girls had all confided that drooling over Luke had inspired them and sent them home, ready to tangle with their husbands. And who could blame them? I felt inspired as well, but I wanted to tangle with the man himself and not the vibrator I'd been using a lot more since I saw him. I just needed a shot of courage first.

"Laci, would you like the usual?" Luke's smooth as silk voice silenced the table full of

women.

I looked up from the menu and found him at our table, an order pad in his hand. How'd he get there so quick? He'd also just used my name, leaving no doubt he remembered exactly who I was.

Audrey shot me an "I got you," look and spoke up. "We're kinda split down the middle on one of your menu items, and we need your input."

"Sure. I'm at your service, ladies." Luke grinned.

He may have addressed everyone, but he was looking at me. His open interest gave me a boost of hope and another swirl of heat in my lower abdomen.

I felt like we had a secret between us. Could Luke and I have another chance to see if the chemistry between us could be mixed and proven viable? I suppressed a giggle at my lame joke.

Yeah, I was still a science nerd.

I caught his raised eyebrow at my not so suppressed laugh, and then he winked at me. Damn. I wiggled in my seat and sucked in a groan as the movement caused me to squeeze my thighs together, putting delicious pressure on my clit.

"Actually, we were all thinking we'd follow Laci's lead this time. You know she likes your Candy Cane hard seltzer and claims it's like a decadent treat or a dessert.

And now you have these yummy key lime cupcakes on the menu, so what are your thoughts on having dessert first?"

"My favorite meal." His gaze stayed on me, and my pussy throbbed at his continued, intense scrutiny. Lord, did he have any idea what he was doing to me without touching me?

A sigh erupted around the table.

"A man after my own heart." Deidre rested her chin on her palm and leaned over the table. "So, is it ever okay to have dessert first before the main course? And of course, birthday cake doesn't count."

"That's right. Birthday cake can be eaten any time." Blayne added.

"Hey, Luke, table six is asking for you—again." A high-pitched voice rang out. It was one of the servers sweeping past our table.

Luke's gaze didn't waver. "I'll be there soon. I'm helping these ladies make an important decision."

Deidre spoke first. "As a matter of fact, it's Laci's birthday next Friday. She's going to be, uh, thirty-something, and we're going to be celebrating—it's gonna be big."

"Big, huh? Sounds fun." He broke our eye contact and turned to Deidre. "Be sure to come in; the first drink is on me. And to answer your question, dessert should always be eaten first."

Once again, his intense gaze on me allayed any doubt that he was speaking directly to me. I shifted again in my seat, searching for relief at his provocative words. Dessert. Eaten. Lord, I had sex on the brain. I guess that tended to happen when you hadn't had a sex partner in over two years, and my vibrator didn't count.

"I'll put in an order for four Candy Canes and have them out to you asap, and you let the server know about those cupcakes. Right now, duty calls. And, Laci, if you're going to be here for a while, let me know. I'd love to catch up."

Our table watched him walk away in silence. All sorts of emotions hit me at once.

"Girl, you know him? Why were you keeping that from us?" Deidre teased.

I was caught. I should have told them, I know, but some things from our past were hard to share. "I wasn't...okay, I was, but I really wasn't sure Luke would remember me. I tutored him in biology for a semester in college before I got pregnant and married Kevin. There's not much to tell—"

Audrey cleared her throat and gave me a look.

I was saved from answering when our drinks were delivered. I took a long sip. Then another.

When it was obvious my friends were waiting for me to talk, I sighed and confessed all.

Deidre and Blayne listened and kept looking from him to me as I told my story. Deidre fanned herself. "He was locked on you. Hard. That, my friend, is a signal from the Universe that you need to go after his fine ass."

"I'd let him play with my ass." Blayne raised her glass of the house IPA and drained its remaining contents.

"Blayne, you're cut off. I've never seen this side of you. You and Lawrence doing okay, you know, in the bedroom?"

"Girl, I'm fine. Lawrence is still fine after nineteen years. But I'm not dead. I know a guaranteed good time when I see one. And Laci, you need to have that good time and then tell us everything. He'll give you your groove back."

"OMG, are we on a reality show right now? Where are the cameras? You all make me sound desperate. I'm not. Just occasionally...horny. I can't believe I just said that. Look, you have all been there for me during my divorce from Kevin and my empty nest breakdown when the girls left for college. And I love you for it, but please, if he comes back over, behave."

"Laci, you're right. You decide, and you know we're here for you no matter what. We just want you happy."

"Happy *and* satisfied. And that man will satisfy you. Just think about it, sweetie. I gotta go.

The boys have an early lacrosse game in the morning." Audrey stood and hugged everyone.

I stepped into her hug when she froze. "No way. Is that Kevin? Laci, that guy Luke is talking to at that table over there looks just like Kevin."

Unbelievable. Fate wouldn't be this cruel twice in a lifetime.

CHAPTER THREE

LUKE

I couldn't believe the old friend from school was Kevin, Laci's ex. And he was just as obnoxious now as he was back then. And he was one drink away from being shitfaced. The group of guys he was with wasn't any better off.

"It was good seeing you, Kevin, but I need to get back. How about I send out a plate of our sliders and potato nachos? You haven't eaten yet, right? I really appreciate your business and stopping by the pub."

I shook his hand and thought I'd made a clean getaway, but Kevin gripped my hand and stood, not too steadily, and faced me. "Hey, did you see that table over there in the corner? It's

Laci with her friends. We're not married anymore, but you remember her, right?"

My hands curled into a fist at the creepy smile on my old roommate's face. I centered my stance and watched as Kevin tried not to sway in front of me. "She fucking kicked me out two years ago. Did you know that? Now she's all dressed up, looking for action, no doubt. Damn, she was so cold when we were married...keep an eye on her for me, would you, and make sure no one hits on her?"

I was surprised at Kevin's swift change from blasting Laci to making sure she was taken care of. Almost made me think twice about going after her, but not quite. She could make up her own mind when I finally got some time alone with her. Which I needed to get Kevin sobered up and out of here so I could make that happen.

"No worries, man. I'll see that she's well taken care of." I slapped him on the back and walked toward the kitchen, and put in the food order. For the next hour, I kept an eye on Kevin and his friends while juggling various requests for either football stories or the brewing process. Once I got Laci's ex out of the pub, I'd head over to her table and make my next play. I would not let another night or a couple of weeks go by without getting her number or setting up a date.

LACI

I turned at Audrey's shocked words, and sure enough, my ex was sitting at a table with a bunch of his buddies, and by the look on Luke's face, he was telling some stupid story. Even though Kevin had moved to Seattle after the divorce, he'd come back often to play golf with his friends. Damn. Damn. Damn.

"I'm sorry, Laci. Do you want me to stay? I don't think he knows you're here; otherwise, he would have come over and made an ass of himself already."

I looked at my best friend, knowing she would stay and

have my back if anything like that happened, but Audrey needed to be home early tonight. "You're sweet, but I can handle him."

"Yeah, we can stay with Laci as long as she wants. We'll make sure that dork doesn't ruin the rest of our evening."

I burst out laughing at Deidre's favorite nickname for my ex because he was a dork. But he was also the father of my girls, so I needed to try to not make waves. Kevin had a habit of sharing our disagreements with them, and I didn't want them drawn into any more drama.

"You two are the best. I just want to finish my drink, and we still need to get those yummy cupcakes, right? Audrey, I'll save you some and bring them over later this weekend, okay?"

She looked at me hard, but then nodded and gave me another hug. "Okay. But don't let this unexpected appearance by Kevin keep you from going after Luke. Promise me."

"Promise." I made a cross over my heart. "Now, go home and get some rest. You're gonna need it to deal with the early game tomorrow. Love you."

She left, and I took another peek toward Luke. Would he come back and talk to me, or would this be like the other nights where the pub got so busy any chance of getting time together would be impossible?

"Okay, here's what we're gonna do. You scoot your chair over a bit more toward the wall, and that way, when the dork leaves, your back will be to him. And we're gonna get those cupcakes and enjoy the rest of the night."

Blayne and Deidre talked me into one more drink, even though I wanted to stay clear-headed, just in case. And, of course, they wanted more time ogling Luke to go with the cupcakes.

Luckily, I didn't have to participate much in the conversation, so it gave me plenty of time to think about what I did want. And I wanted orgasms, lots of them. I missed the intensity of a shared physical release, of touch and taste and hot breath against sensitized skin, and...I tried to stay focused on the conversation, but I couldn't stop thinking about being with Luke and what it would be like. My ex had never been interested in my pleasure after the twins had been born, and it'd gone downhill from there.

An hour of fantasizing passed when Deidre grabbed my hand. "Don't turn around. The ex is leaving with his dork pack."

My ex always had unfortunate timing; because, of course, he would be around on the night I wanted to let Luke know I wanted him. But I would not let history repeat itself. I kept myself still and stared out the window into the parking lot, repeating the mantra to myself, *"keep walking, keep walking."* And thank God it worked. Kevin was wrapped up in impressing his friends as they lumbered out of the pub.

"Okay, all clear." Deidre sighed and rubbed my arm. "You okay?"

I was now. I looked at my watch. Four more hours till closing, I wasn't sure I could make it.

My late night, or rather early morning hours of partying, were well in my past.

"You know, he keeps looking over here, right?"

Blayne's words had me worried. Did Kevin come back in? "Who?"

"Who do you think? Luke. He may be talking to his customers, but his attention is all on you."

Deidre sighed. There seemed to be a lot of that going on

tonight. "So, are you going to go over there and talk to him or what? Because I don't want to leave until you do."

"Hold on, wait...yes, here he comes. Act natural."

Act natural? I let out a snort and finished the last of my drink. Okay, I could do this. There was no way I was going to let another two weeks go by, dammit.

"Hi, ladies. How'd those cupcakes taste? Not too much key lime flavoring, I hope."

I felt my face warm. Hopefully, he couldn't tell what I was thinking every time I looked at him. Like having his tongue taste me, and how I wanted to taste him?

The corner of Luke's mouth lifted, and his gaze fell to my glass, where I'd been rubbing my finger around its rim as I fantasized. Yeah, I had it bad.

"No, they're perfect. Thanks for stopping by and checking up on us. Laci just told us you two went to college together. That's so cool. You two wanted to catch up, right, Deidre?" Blayne

gave Deidre a look, and both women quickly grabbed their purses and stood to leave.

"Well, ladies, thank you for coming in tonight. I hope we'll see you again soon?" Luke helped both Blayne and Deidre with their coats. My friends were all over that offer.

"Oh, this is our favorite place, and I'm sure we'll be in soon. Isn't that right, Laci?"

I was never comfortable being the center of attention, and now there were three sets of eyes on me as I bent down under the table for my purse. Awkward. Tearing my gaze from Luke, I grabbed my bag. The movement pulled my blouse down, and for a moment, I was on full display thanks to my newly purchased push-up bra.

A heated flush crept up my neck. My gaze was drawn back to Luke's. His eyes were no longer on my face but on my chest, and reading his look, he was very interested. It was a definite boost to my ego. I'd been blessed with or cursed, depending on the day and the outfit, large breasts.

Luke's attention on me felt good and ignited a new level of determination.

"Ahem." Deidre cleared her throat. "I see we're not needed here, so Laci, um—we'll see you next Friday?"

Blayne giggled and placed a hand on Luke's arm. "Our girl here needs a distraction. A big one. You up for the task?"

"Blayne!" I wanted to crawl under the table, yet desperately wanted to hear his answer because his eyes hadn't left me since he walked over. "You don't have to answer that. She's

usually not so forward."

"No, it's fine. If you don't ask, you might miss out on something pretty awesome, right,

Laci?" I nodded. My mouth had gone dry, and my nipples hardened from his throaty response.

My friends were grinning like fools, and each sent me an exaggerated wink before they said their goodbyes and left me with Luke.

Now alone, the roomful of people faded as I focused intently on the man I never thought I'd have a chance with again. I was not missing this gift handed to me.

"I'm closing tonight if you want to come in later? Things usually calm down around 1 a.m., if that's not too late. I've been slammed with business. I've been working every day since we opened; otherwise, I'd ask you to dinner, but I don't know when I'll be able to get away. If you can't, I understand, but I'd really like to catch up. Maybe have a nightcap and reminisce about college. I wanted to talk to you last week, but by the time the crowd thinned out, you had left."

He had? "I'd like that." My over-enthusiastic response had me groaning inwardly as my pulse raced. *Way to go, Laci, desperate much?*

"Great. That's great...I'll see you later." Luke leaned in and kissed my forehead, and squeezed my arm.

The husky timbre in his voice and his touch vibrated through me—one a.m. couldn't come quick enough. I wanted to say something that conveyed my true feelings, but my brain was all scrambled by his closeness, so I gave him a short wave and did my best not to trip on my way out the door.

I may no longer know how to flirt or talk to a hot guy today any more than I had back in college when he'd been sitting across from me in the library, but there was no way I was going to miss out on letting him know exactly how I felt about him, then and now.

CHAPTER FOUR

LACI

The parking lot was half full when I pulled into a space right up front at 12:58 a.m. I'd taken a power nap and set an alarm to wake me half an hour before I wanted to leave. Sitting there, I took a moment before getting out of my car and recalled the last night Luke and I had seen each other. I was moving out of my dorm, and he had just heard about Kevin getting me pregnant.

How I wished it had been him. The entire time he stammered out his goodbye, I kept my gaze on anything but him. My heart felt ten sizes too big, and my stomach roiled from constant nausea. It was a memory I wish I didn't have, and I'm not too proud to say I've thought about that moment over the years. Typically, after another blowout with Kevin and I would sink into regret that I hadn't told Luke that night how I felt, how I wanted him to be my first.

A group of twenty-something's exited the pub. Their laughter rang loud and merry. I envied their freedom, the ability to live life from one moment to the next. Well, I was here to do the same thing.

I got out of my car, locked it with my remote, and stopped short. He was just inside the doorway, holding it open for me. The look on his face, the crooked smile, slammed me right back to college and dreaming about that look after a night of tutoring. But tonight, tonight was different. We were different. We still had a connection, but we were seeing each other through different lenses with a lifetime behind us. Well, at least I was. And this time, I wasn't going home wishing I'd been honest with him. And I was all in.

I hope he was ready for the new Laci.

"Laci. I'm not ashamed to admit; I worried you wouldn't come." Luke held the door as I stepped past him. His scent drifted over me—a mixture of hops and man with a hint of sandalwood. I was on sensory overload as I took in another deep breath to even myself out.

"You said 1 a.m. was best, right?" Turning in a slow circle to take in the room and its few remaining customers, my gaze didn't quite reach his as I realized he'd changed his clothes since I'd left earlier. His hair was damp, and his shirt clung to his body, outlining his pecs and broad shoulders. And his arms. Arms I'd fantasize about wrapped around me as we sat across from each other in the college library.

"Um, Laci. You okay?" Luke's eyes shone with concern.

Holding back a laugh, I nodded. "I'm great. I, uh, just had a quick thought. I'd forgotten to, uh, lock my front door, but then I remembered I did, so..." *Lame, so lame, Laci.*

"Front door huh, well, okay. If you say so." Luke looked me up and down; his grin was a knowing one. Like knowing I'd been checking him out and got caught. "I'm glad you're here.

How about we sit in the back while we catch up and pray no one needs me for the hour?"

He led the way to a corner of the pub tucked behind a six-foot room divider made of roughhewn wood and stained dark to match the flooring. Padded booths in black leather with brass studs, arranged in a U shape, with three large tables filling the middle. Short, fat candles were placed at various intervals, an amber glow giving the space a cozy, intimate feel.

"This is our VIP area. I thought we could hang out here uninterrupted and talk." He swept out an arm indicating the far side, and another waft of his cologne hit me. It was addicting and comforting and sexy as hell. It, combined with the man, had me sitting anywhere he wanted me.

After asking what I'd like to drink, he excused himself for a moment and returned with his beer and my hard seltzer, as well as a glass of water. I knew my limits, and I wanted no doubts about anything I would say or do tonight to be in question or blamed on having over-imbibed.

"Thank you. This pub is fantastic, by the way. My friends don't want to go anywhere else now for our girls' nights." I took a small sip of my seltzer for fortification and looked over at Luke.

He was sitting sideways with his body toward me, an ankle over his leg and an arm resting on a knee. So close, in fact, if I shifted to my left, I'd be snuggled right up to his thigh. His body heat warmed me as I tried to focus on his responses, but all I could think about was that I was hidden away with Luke.

I was free to say and do anything I wanted for the first time in way too long.

"I'm glad your friends like the place. But what about you? What do you think?" He took a drink and kept his gaze on mine as he swallowed. The move was so sexy I felt my body heat at the desire I found in his brown eyes.

Smiling, I didn't want to tip off my excitement at being able to see him every other Friday night. "Well, who am I to argue? Majority rules and all."

"Always the rule follower, weren't you?" He laughed while I frowned. "No, no. Now don't give me that look. I remember that look of disappointment whenever I tried to end our tutoring sessions early. And by the way, there'll be no ducking out early for me tonight. I want to hear all about you."

Luke's voice had gone another notch lower on the word 'you.' I shivered at the emphasis and tried not to wish away all the years between then and now. Things happened for a reason. Who knows, if we had hooked up back then, we were both so young there was no guarantee we'd have

had any kind of lasting relationship.

But now. Older and wiser, and all of that could equal a chance at something better.

We spent the next hour talking about my girls, the decision to stay in town, how Kevin and I drifted apart, then only stayed married for the kids and our inevitable divorce. I kept the fact that by the end of the marriage, we were in separate rooms a secret or the fact that I was terrified of turning into a shriveled-up divorcee before I turned forty.

He told me about being drafted by the Washington Sentinels, his career-ending injury, and how he turned his love of small-batch brewing into his award-winning Hart's Pass IPA and building the brewery back here in our hometown.

Before I'd found the courage to let him know about the

fateful night I'd given my virginity to Kevin and not him as I'd hoped, the lead bartender interrupted us.

"Hey, boss. The till's taken care of, the place is cleared, and all the servers are clocked out.

You want me to set the alarm or..." The young tattooed employee looked between us and waited for direction. He looked uncomfortable, and it made me wonder if this situation happened often.

Were the rumors true? Was this back area used as Luke's typical end-of-night hook-up?

And why did I care? After all, that's why I came back so late. I was totally out of my comfort zone, but I was also determined. I sat up a bit straighter. "Oh, I'd really like to keep talking. That is if you don't have anywhere else to be?"

In all our time tonight, the mention of a girlfriend had never come up, but I'd made it plain to him that I was single. I crossed my fingers under the table and waited for his response.

He nodded at his employee. "Go ahead. I've got it tonight," his gaze quickly returned to mine as we both seemed to hold our breath, waiting to hear the back door close, ensuring we were truly alone.

His eyes were now hooded as he looked back at me. He didn't move closer, but I felt a shift occur in each of us as a possible scenario played out in my mind.

It seemed like forever before he spoke again. "You're so beautiful, Laci. More so now than the shy but determined girl you once were. And don't get me wrong, you were pretty then, but you were off-limits to me. You know that, right?"

My head swam at his words. Off-limits? What in the world was he talking about? Had Kevin warned him off?

Luke leaned toward me and caught a wayward curl of mine in his hands. His fingers brushed my chest as he rubbed the hair between his finger and thumb. "Coach threatened me with my scholarship if I started anything with you. He said the team had had too many players 'defiling' tutors in the past, and he'd be damned if I fell out of the program and possibly lose my chances with the NFL if I so much as kissed you on the cheek."

I remained frozen at the news. Was this his way of telling me he'd been attracted to me in college? That some stupid football coach had blocked my chances with Luke?

"You were so sweet and untouchable, Laci. And those damn tight jeans you wore. I don't mind telling you now... since we're older, but jeez, you were so hot I'd have to rub one out in the

shower after our sessions and—"

The sound of breaking glass interrupted Luke. We both looked over to the bar where the noise had seemed to come from. It was the bartender. He was back, and his face was beet red. He looked like he was going to bolt.

"Shit. I thought you'd left." Luke strode over and helped his employee clean up the mess. "I forgot my sweatshirt. I'd left it under the bar, and there must have been a forgotten glass under there, so when I pulled it...I'm so sorry, boss."

Luke's employee looked at me. "Sorry, ma'am. I didn't mean to wreck your...I mean the moment between you two—"

Luke growled. "That's enough. You've got most of it. I'll see you tomorrow."

I've never seen a person disappear as quickly as I did the poor bartender. I stood up to help Luke with the remaining mess. I had a hard time not laughing at the situation. The guy couldn't have picked the worst time. "I hope you're not too mad at him. It seems like an honest accident.

Wait, can an accident be honest? Well, whatever. Let me help you before I go."

I stepped up on the brass foot railing and peeked over the bar top to see Luke sweeping up the last of the glass into a dustpan.

"You're leaving?" He didn't sound very happy about it.

"Um, maybe...it's late and..."

"Hold on. Don't leave. Let me take care of this." Luke disappeared into the back.

Standing alone in a darkened pub wanting to climb Luke like a tree even though I still hadn't told him my truth was an unusual place to be. How could I get the intimate vibe going again? Because after Luke telling me about jerking off because he couldn't touch me back then, well, that was the type of news a girl didn't walk away from.

I was still debating how to seduce Luke when he strode back into the main room from the back. There was purpose and determination in his stride as he stopped in front of me. Less than an inch separated us. I leaned back against the edge of the bar, looking up into his heated gaze. I was mesmerized by his intense gaze and then I didn't think anymore. I simply acted.

I grabbed his shoulders and pulled myself up on my tiptoes and kissed him. Soft at first, until he groaned, and his hands circled my waist, lifting me to sit on the bar top. He stepped between my legs and took control of the kiss. Deep and hot, our tongues tangled, dueling for control. I let go first, and he captured and sucked my bottom lip before his hands burrowed into my hair, holding either side of my head, giving me everything he had into our first kiss. It was heaven, and sin rolled into the most erotic kiss I'd ever experienced, and I wanted more.

Breathing soon became an issue, and he slowed the kiss down so we could take deep gulps of air. I pulled my body closer to his, wrapping my legs tight around his back and hooking my ankles. I wasn't letting him go anywhere.

"Damn. Laci...I..." Luke let out a shallow laugh and then groaned as I rubbed my chest against his.

"I know me too. I thought maybe we could make up for lost time." Looking into his dark eyes, I licked his lips, nipped the bottom of his lower lip, then kissed it better. "I want you, Luke.

Just in case there's any doubt. I want you to touch, lick, and fuck me. Right now."

I watched as his eyes dilated, and the already hard erection I was cradling between my thighs seemed to grow and began pulsing. I reached down and stroked him through his jeans. "This is what I wanted that night at the frat party. It was never Kev—" I let out a squeak as he kissed me hard, released my waist, then began unbuttoning my blouse.

"Thank fuck, a front clasping bra." He made quick work of the push-up bra I had bought with him in mind and freed my achy breasts. He cupped each one and massaged my sensitive flesh and rubbed his thumbs over my nipples.

"No more mention of your ex, deal? This is about us."

I nodded as heat spiraled in my core, and I felt my panties become soaked. The need for him to touch me increased as he kissed me again until we were panting. He trailed his lips down my neck until he captured one of my rock-hard nipples into his hot mouth. "Luke, yes. Please touch me." I guided one of his hands to my thigh and pushed it onto my mound. I lifted my hips.

"Here, touch me here."

"You're pretty bossy." He released my nipple and looked up at me with a wicked grin. "I like it, don't stop. Anything you want me to touch, I'll do it twice."

Entranced by the desire I saw in his eyes. I had a moment of 'is this really happening?' Me, sitting on a bar in the dark having sex with the man of my dreams. How did I get so lucky?

"I-I'm not usually like this; in fact, it's been, well, it's been a long time. But with you, this seems right."

He looked at me for a long time, our bodies still touching, our breathing heavy. The anticipation of his next touch was agony. "Laci, sweetheart, I agree. It is right, and I'm going to make this so good for you."

Luke captured my breasts again, held my gaze as he slowly circled my nipples, driving me insane. "You're so responsive it's killing me—the things I want to do to you right now. Shit, tell me you want it all because I'll stop now if you need me to. Not that I want to, but baby, you are too tempting right now for me to go much longer."

"I guess you missed the part where I said I want you to fuck me, Luke. Because I do so very much." The words came out so naturally. I was amazed at my brazenness, but God, I wanted nothing more than every way he could have me, right here, right now.

He gifted me with the most brilliant of smiles. "Oh, I'm going to fuck you, Laci Monroe. But first I'm going to do some tasting. Because I also remember you saying you want me to lick you, and I'm going to spread you wide and lick you till you scream my name."

His lips returned to mine, and he swallowed my 'yes.' I felt his fingers tunnel under the sides of my panties as he tugged them down. Cool air hit my core, and I moaned. I wiggled my hips as he dragged the lace down my thighs and past my shoes.

He leaned down to my stomach and began dropping kisses down to my pussy as I leaned back and braced my hands on the bar top. I opened every part of myself to him and his wicked tongue. He grasped my thighs and opened me wide.

"So pretty, and so wet. Just for me." He blew on my exposed skin, and I jumped at the sensation. "Hold on, baby."

The first lick had me jerking forward. *"Yyyes!"* I breathed out.

The second was slower. Deeper. *Oh, my god.*

The third, he dived between my folds and stayed and began a rhythm that had me rocking my hips. I grabbed the back of his head and rode his tongue. The pressure of an orgasm built. I felt my inner walls spasm and tighten on his tongue as he lapped up my juices. When he took my clit into his mouth and sucked me, I lost it. "More, god yes, Luke. That feels sooo good."

He released me, and I whimpered, but he immediately began flicking my bundle of nerves and slipped a finger inside me, fucking me with his finger as his tongue danced me to the best orgasm of my life.

I screamed his name and begged him not to stop. I pinched my nipples as he first suckled my inner lips and tunneled his tongue inside me. The sense of time and place left me. All I knew was this moment, the pressure and pleasure of his flesh as he brought me to another level of fulfillment.

My hips rocked as his tongue continued to fuck me as another sharp wave was building within me. I lifted my hips, pressing myself closer. His tongue consumed me. The intense contact ignited another flash of fire throughout me, pooling in my center. My legs fell open wider, allowing him full access, permitting him to go as deep as he could with his wicked tongue.

I whispered his name over and over. On the crest of another explosive orgasm, I held on. The thrumming of his lips on my swollen flesh and the long licks of his tongue prolonged the orgasm as my body quivered.

I was...done, convinced he'd wrung every last ounce of decadence from me. And yet, I didn't want this to end. And as if he could read my thoughts as well as he played my flesh, tears came to my eyes, his talented finger still buried deep inside me, tapped my g-spot. "Luke! Oh.

My. Fucking. God. Yes!" A growl escaped me as I finally let the orgasm crest and fall. I gulped for breath as he finished lapping up my juices. I'd never been so wet or so well satisfied.

I let my limbs go limp and sighed. Was this really happening? Spread out wide on top of the bar, a row of tiny lights along the length of the mirror, creating an atmosphere of hedonism I could quickly become addicted to. There was no doubt I had just experienced the hottest sex not even my wildest fantasies could conjure.

"Do you want me to keep going?" Luke's husky voice and hot breath fanned my overheated skin just above my pubic bone.

I looked down at his devilish grin and returned his smile with one of my own. I couldn't speak. Keep going? Hell, yeah. I nodded and watched him; I was beyond turned on.

He flicked my clit with his tongue. "So pretty and pink. And wet. I'm thinking I need at least another taste before my cock demands its turn inside your sweet and tight pussy. Tell me what you want, Laci."

What did I want? He'd given me something I'd no idea existed. He made me feel free enough to request anything. But how could I top two orgasms?

Could I? I'd never cum twice in a row—ever. Not even with my vibrator. Hell, my ex had never tried to get me off more than once, and sadly, it was the rare occasion when I came at all.

Did I dare ask for just one more amazing "O" before I took care of him? I had the sudden urge to take him deep between my lips and give him the same satisfaction he'd given me.

For a moment, where we were hit me, and that anyone could have looked in any of the uncovered windows sent a thrill through me. Sure, it was late, but what if someone came back looking for a lost item and found us fucking on the bar top instead? Truth be told, I no longer cared. I just wanted...him.

I'd never had sex outside of a bedroom, but now that I had and the excitement, the potential of being caught or someone watching us ignited a new sensation within me. It was equal parts frightening, exhilarating, and freeing. I looked around, and I froze when my gaze landed on a security camera.

Luke noticed my reaction and squeezed my thigh. "Don't worry. I'll delete the recording.

After we're done."

Nodding, I sat up and wrapped my arms around his neck.

"Darlin', I'm just getting started. Now, how about you let me turn you over so I can lick you till you come again before I fuck you till you scream my name? I like the sound of it on your lips."

I'd barely nodded yes before he grabbed me around my waist and turned me to face the mirror. I scrambled to gain balance on my knees, the anticipation of what was next overwhelmed me. Our gazes clashed in our mirrored reflection. My shirt hung open, some of the buttons were missing, and my skirt was hiked up around my waist. My skin was flushed pink, and my breasts swayed from the sudden movement.

Luke let out a groan and cupped my flesh. "Look at you, Laci. You're so fucking hot with your hair wild around your face. And your beautiful tits. Damn, your nipples are just begging to be sucked again, aren't they, baby?"

He flicked the tips and pinched both as I stared, mesmerized, at the picture we made. God, I wanted everything he described and more. His words made my pussy clench and throb. I never thought I'd enjoy dirty talk, but it turned me on, and I wanted more of it. So much more.

"Don't worry, baby. They'll have a turn soon. Right now, I just need to bury my face between your sweet ass and lick that pussy again. You taste so damn sweet, candycane sweet.

Just like I knew you would that first day I saw you."

"Th-the first day?" My breath hitched at his words.

"Hell, yes. You were so shy as you checked me out. And you were checking me out, weren't you, Laci? Wondering what it would be like between us?"

I nodded. I had. And now I knew. At least some of what it would be like, but I wanted it all. I licked my lips. I wanted to know what he tasted like, too. "I want to go down on you, Luke."

"Later. You suck me now, and I won't be able to keep from going off." He slid his hands down my arms and placed them over my hands and guided me onto the lower section of the bar, below to where the drinks were made. He stretched me out and made sure I was steady, then ran his hands back over my arms, my shoulders, and down my back until he reached my bottom. I was on the verge of coming again simply from having his hands on me. Moving, I tried to find relief.

"I need your ass high up in the air for me. There you go, just like that. Now I'm going to spread your thighs a bit...ah, fuck me, so damn pretty, baby."

His words made me shudder, and my pussy spasmed. My nipples, if possible, became harder.

I moved a hand to pinch one. Luke slapped my ass, and I almost came from the sweet pain of it. After a moment of shock, I quickly decided I liked it, and I needed to come again. I quickly tunneled between my legs and touched my clit, now engorged from the sting of the slap.

Before I could rub it a second time, Luke tapped my hand over my swollen bud, and another delicious curl of heat pooled. I let out a squeal. Where had my inner vixen been all these years? I fucking loved this.

"No touching. That's my job." Luke rubbed back and forth from my clit to the edge of my hole. Then he'd flick my swollen flesh and started over. Overwhelmed by the sensations, I stretched my back and dipped my head low, and took in the flow of new pleasures he was creating.

"Look at yourself, Laci. Look and see how beautiful, how fucking sexy you are." Luke's tongue followed his words.

I did look at myself in the mirror and almost didn't recognize the woman I saw there. Raw, half-naked, and turned on beyond belief. I watched as Luke dived behind me and licked until I screamed his name over and over.

When I attempted to move and bounce up and down on his tongue, he locked me in place with his large hands and nipped my clit. Another orgasm built at the contact, and I held onto to the moment as his tongue crept further back. But he moved again and pressed a thumb onto my clit, extending this orgasm until I almost passed out.

"Luke, yes!"

I couldn't believe the sound of my voice as I came and dripped onto Luke's face. He pressed

even harder on my pussy with his nose, and my legs shook at the pressure.

"Baby, can I touch your asshole? Just the outside. I won't go further unless you tell me it's okay."

I locked my legs and wanted to say yes, but I'd never liked anal sex. The one time I'd tried it, it had not gone well, and I'd avoided it from then on. But with Luke, maybe... maybe it would be

different. He made me feel so good and feel things I had no idea I could feel.

He was waiting for permission. The idea of it created another flood of warmth inside me. Maybe if I touched myself while he did it, it would feel better than before? Because tonight Luke made me want to test myself.

Explore all the pleasure I could handle.

Listen to him talk dirty to me and talk dirty back.

His hand moved back toward my pussy —

"No! I mean, yes. I want that. I want to...to try. Please, Luke."

Another groan tore from him. "I'm going to touch you

first with my fingers, my thumbs. I'm going to take your juices and lube you up, and ah, yes, there you go. I just want to play. Nothing too deep. We'll save that for next time."

Next time? Was there going to be another chance to do this again?

Luke tapped my flesh and circled the opening; the sensation overwhelmed me.

"How's that feel, baby? You okay?"

I couldn't speak, so I nodded and began fingering myself and rotating my hips, trying to find another release. This was fucking insane. Who was I right now? God, I'd never felt this horny in my life, and he hadn't even put his cock inside me yet.

"That's it, baby, just keep stroking. Damn, watching you touch yourself is making me so hard. I need to be inside you. Hold on." Luke scooped me off the bar, and I wrapped my legs around his waist. He strode over to the closed-off section where we'd been earlier.

"I'm sorry, I can't wait." He gently placed me on the tabletop and took a step back. When he lifted his shirt over his head, my jaw dropped.

Damn. I knew he'd been a professional ballplayer, but he was ripped and toned, as if he was still actively playing. My hands went to his abs and followed the hard lines of his muscles as he unbuckled his belt, unzipped his jeans, and freed his cock.

I blinked at the beauty of the man standing before me. Long and thick with a bead of pre-cum on its tip, his cock jutted toward my face as I reached out.

"Not now, baby. Next time."

Again, with next time. We were going to need to talk about that because I'd planned for just one night with him. After tonight, there would be no coming back to his pub. I knew the score with Luke. I'd heard the rumors about him. And he didn't date. He fucked. And that was fine with me. It's what I'd wanted.

For my birthday. And lucky me, I got my present early.

"Lie back down for me." Luke held my gaze as he produced a condom, rolled it on, and kicked his jeans to the side.

Finally, he was going to be inside me.

CHAPTER FIVE

LUKE

Fuck, she was perfect. Laci's sexy curves and confidence in her body, and what she wanted from me, had me on the edge of coming. I knew I was an ass for taking her on the table in the VIP area. She deserved better, but she was so fucking hot thinking straight was no longer possible. I had a double-wide lounger in my office, but I knew I couldn't make it there.

"Luke?"

Uncertainty covered Laci's beautiful face. "Don't worry. I haven't changed my mind. Before I fill you up, I wanted to look at you.

I'd waited so long for this moment. The weight of it finally lifted from my chest, and I groaned at the naughty grin on her face.

"Luke, hurry. I want, no, I need you inside me."

"Shit, Laci." I grabbed my shaft and lined myself up to her wet pussy, and entered her inch by sweet inch. When I was fully inside her, I dropped to my elbows and braced myself on either side of her. "Hold on, baby."

With each stroke, I watched her face as she took all of me. She raised her knees, and I

thought I'd go blind as I went deeper and began pounding into her. She held my gaze and

squeezed my cock with each thrust.

"Fuck, that feels good." I dipped my thumb down to her clit and rubbed her sweet bundle as she moved beneath, seeking another release.

"Luke, please. I'm..."

"So wet for me, yeah, cum for me, baby." I flicked her as she came undone under me and rocked into her twice more before I followed and came as she cried out my name. Having my name on her sweet lips and her inner walls squeezing my cock prolonged my orgasm.

"Laci," I whispered her name and dropped kisses on her forehead and eyes before taking her lips in a slow open-mouthed kiss as our bodies settled from the intense pleasure. Her hips continued to buck. "Sweetheart, you gotta know how damn good that was."

Her breaths were slowing down, and she gave me a shy smile. "It was, wasn't it?"

"Hell, yeah." I gave her another kiss. "I'm going to pick you up, and then we're going back to my office. I have a large couch there and would have gone in there, but I couldn't wait. We'll clean up and rest for a bit, okay?"

I noticed a slight change in her eyes at my words, but I let it go. We hadn't talked about anything beyond the moment of getting our hands on each other, so it kind of made sense she was now unsure about what came next.

Striding with Laci in my arms toward the back of the pub, I planned on changing that very soon. Just as soon as I

recovered from finally being where I've wanted to be for twenty fucking
    years.

～

LACI

After Luke took care of the condom and then sweetly took a warm cloth and cleaned us both up in his bathroom, he picked me up again and laid me down on the widest couch I'd ever seen in an office. He got behind me, and we spooned in silence for a bit. It was nice. My body needed the recovery time before I headed home.

"I wasn't telling you the whole truth earlier." Luke's growly voice tickled my ear.

His tone was laced with truth and sin as he massaged my arm and hip. My mind didn't know whether to rejoice at his welcomed touch or to put up shields to protect myself from a confession I may not like.

Luke owed me nothing. I walked into his place tonight with the complete understanding that we'd be scratching a 20-year itch. But I had been holding on to a small kernel of hope that our intense physical connection would bloom into more.

He nipped my ear and blew softly to lessen the sting. Instead, it ramped me up. He'd already discovered earlier when he was inside me how sensitive I was and that the simple act of blowing in my ear was one of my erogenous zones. I pumped my hips and tucked my backside into his groin. Maybe if I distracted him, we'd have another round. He'd recovered quickly and was hard
    again as he thrust his cock into my ass.

"Your little game of distraction isn't going to keep me from telling you a few more things before I drag myself away from your luscious body and find another condom so I can fuck you again." Luke slapped my butt cheek then rubbed it lightly, creating another level of play I didn't know I wanted.

"Be good, and you'll get exactly what you're begging for."

Yes, please. I want this and so much more from him, but I wanted him to tell me his truth before I shared mine. "Luke, I have no idea what you're talking about. I was just stretch—"

A low chuckle erupted from his chest. The rumble caressed my back and offered me the hope I was looking for.

"Now, where was I? Oh, yeah..." He wound his hand between our bodies and began to tease my flesh.

"Luke!" The light touch had me lifting myself off the couch. My God, it hurt so good, as my over-stimulated flesh practically wept for him to do it again.

"Now that I have your attention, I wanted to make sure you knew that I was aware that you still lived in town and were divorced when I decided to build the brewery and pub here. And if you hadn't come in when you did, I planned on tracking you down. I knew there would be a chance you'd tell me to get lost, but if you remember from college, I like a good challenge."

Luke kissed the crook of my neck and ever so gently pushed his middle finger into me and sweetly tortured me.

"I - I, ooh...so good." Panting, I licked my lips and tried

again to put a coherent thought together. "So, does uh, that mean tonight isn't a one and done for you?"

He ignored me and continued to tease me. In and out, his pace continued slowly, working me into a frenzy. I almost cried out for him to stop when he surprised me and pressed and circled my clit till I almost forgot to breathe.

"Oh, I'm far from done with you, Laci. In fact, I would bet we're meant to be and that…no, *this* was something worth waiting for."

As I fell over the edge once more, I loudly agreed.

EPILOGUE

Six months had passed since the night Luke and I ruined each other for anyone else. He'd met Jennifer and Emma over spring break. I made sure they knew how important Luke was in my life, but not to go planning a wedding quite yet. I'd had one marriage go bad, and I wanted Luke to be sure this was it for him. He'd never married or had kids, and this would be asking a

lot of a man to become part of a ready-made family.

We'd been dating, for lack of a better word, since the first night we had sex in his pub. Every chance we got to be together, we took. It was like we were desperately trying to make up for lost time. I wasn't complaining, but I also knew it wasn't exactly sustainable. The last few times we got together, we'd both fallen asleep on the couch as we watched a movie at my house. Clothes still on when we woke the next morning. Had the excitement of being together finally run its course?

But today was different. We were having a party at the house for my girls with some of their friends to celebrate the end of their first year of college. Both Luke and I would have our friends over too, as it was the first time we'd be seen as an official couple.

But damn if history wasn't repeating itself. Only this time, it was with the right guy, but the timing sucked.

I looked down at the double lines and let out a laugh and a weird hiccup.

Pregnant. I was thirty-seven. I had two adult daughters. Two daughters I had made sure were on birth control from the age of sixteen, and here I was—knocked up—again.

But there was one big difference from the last time I found out I was pregnant. I was head over heels in love with Luke. I just had no idea how he was going to feel about having a baby with me.

Jeez, could I handle going through all the sleepless nights, diaper changes, and fifth-grade math again?

"Laci? You in there, babe?" Luke rattled the door handle. "Sweetheart, people are starting to show up and—"

I unlocked the bathroom door and shoved the stick with two little pink lines in front of his face. "I'm pregnant." I burst into tears.

Luke took the stick from me and wrapped his arms around me as I blubbered into my hands.

I couldn't make eye contact. I wouldn't be able to handle seeing disappointment on his face.

When he merely held me and rubbed my back without saying anything, I took a few deep breaths and forced myself to stop crying. I looked up and found him staring back at me with a goofy smile on his face.

"Two lines, Luke. I thought we'd been so careful. I'm sorry—"

"Babe. I know."

"...things have been so hectic at work and the girls, and I lost track of my period. I think I'm a couple of months along, but I'll have to go to the doctor to verify. And we never talked about

kids or—"

"Laci, slow down. I know, and I'm happy. Thrilled. You've been a bit more tired and complaining about some achiness, so I kinda hoped you were, but I googled some stuff, and believe me, I'd kept track of that time of the month, so—"

My jaw dropped open, and I stared at the man I'd fallen in love with, telling me he'd googled stuff and knew I was pregnant before I did? What the... "Wait, wait, wait a minute. You suspected I was pregnant but never brought it up, and...and you want this baby? You're not mad?"

Luke shook his head, and it was then I noticed his eyes had welled up. "Babe, I know we didn't talk about kids. Please don't worry. I want this baby. I never saw myself with a kid, but hell, with you, I do. I love you so damn much. I was going to give this to you last month, but then I suspected a couple of weeks ago you might be pregnant, so I waited until you figured it out."

In a daze, I watched as Luke pulled a tiny box out of his back pocket and held it out for me. He looked so funny holding it and the pregnancy test in the other hand. "Is that what I think it is?" Tears began pooling in my eyes, and I quickly wiped them away before they could fall.

He set the stick down on the counter, opened the box, took out the ring, and grabbed my hand. "Marry me, Laci. I love you. I love Jennifer and Emma, and I'll even put up with Kevin as long as I can be with you and our child."

"Yes! I love you, Luke." I started crying again as he pulled me in close and kissed me deep.

The sound of the door shutting and the click of the lock broke through my fog of happiness.

"What are you doing? We need to go tell the girls and—"

"Later. Much later. Right now, all I want is the sound of you coming and screaming my name." Luke lifted my arms and took my top off and made quick work of my bra. He took my tender breasts in his hands and placed soft kisses on each one before pinching my nipples until I groaned. He dropped to his knees, pulled down my Capri's, my panties, and kissed and licked me—everything and everyone else forgotten.

I sighed. "Oh, Mr. Hart, you do know exactly what I like."

"Babe, I have twenty years to make up for."

TANGLING WITH THE COWBOY

Jana Bennett
At thirty-four, I'm focused on getting my grandfather's horse ranch back to its former glory. I don't have time to play house or raise babies, and when I have an itch, I scratch it.

Only it's been a while since someone made me want to scratch until an old enemy comes back into my life—and my fantasies.

Lawson Bridges
A former bronco riding rodeo champ returns home with a trunk full of buckles looking for his next challenge.

He finds two.

The first is signing on to run a horse ranch for the woman he couldn't forget.

And the second?

The woman he couldn't forget.

We've been circling each other for years. After sharing an unexpected, yet inevitable, night of passion, can we overcome old wounds and see that we're better together?

CHAPTER ONE

JANA

It had been a month since my world turned upside down, and I was still in shock.

Returning to my hometown, to my grandfather's ranch, had always been at my choosing. Receiving the news that grandad had passed, that he'd kept the severity of his cancer from me, the severity of his financial troubles was, is, a reality I had never expected.

When I left for college, I thought he'd always be there to come home to when and if I needed him. Back then, his horse breeding operation was solid, in reputation and financial security. But the last five years or so, time I wish I had back, had not been kind to him.

Wrapped up in my career, I had been living as far from the ranch life as one could get without leaving the state. Between the crusty ranch hands and small-town gossips, I'd had my fill of small-town life.

The life and the career I'd built were fading away

quicker than the setting sun on a cold winter night. Figuring out how to save Bennett Ranch and the decades old breeding operation weighed heavy and robbed me of not only sleep but hope that what my grandfather had worked so hard for wouldn't disappear mere months after his passing.

As I drove into Cedar Ridge, a small farming and ranch community in northern Idaho, I did my best to ignore the ache in my heart and the anger in my soul for ignoring the warning signs over the years, no matter how small.

Unknown to me, granddad's unscrupulous manager had taken advantage of a weak old man too prideful to call his granddaughter for help. There had been little I could do about the embezzling thief who'd vanished the day after granddad's passing. The local sheriff was doing what he could to track him down and promised me he'd keep looking. But little good it would do in a few months when the balloon payment was due on the mortgage my grandfather had refinanced five years ago. From what I could tell in the mess that was the filing system, he'd done it to cover increasing feed and medical costs and to purchase two additional studs and four mares bronco riders clamored after year after year to produce prize winning foals.

Grandad's dream was now fading fast, and I needed to come up with a hail Mary or it'd be lost to developers, like Archer King, who even now was buying up the surrounding land, turning single family farms and ranches into track housing.

Upon reaching the edge of town, I did my best to clear my head of as much negativity as I could. It wasn't going to do me anything but lose more sleep. Time was running out, but I had a couple ideas to save the ranch. I promised myself nothing but positive thoughts as reached the one and only traffic signal in town.

I narrowed my gaze on the line of cars waiting for the signal to turn green. It was a sight unheard of just a few years ago. Signs were everywhere that the town was booming. The feed store was getting an addition and a new strip mall's foundation was being poured across the street, where an empty lot had been on the market for as long as I could remember.

I zipped through all my errands and pulled up to the Sunrise Diner. It was a favorite stop not to be missed on any trip into town ever since I was a little girl.

"Hi, Sally. Could I get a latte to go?" I looked wistfully at the pastry display case at the far end of the countertop.

"Sure thing, Jana. Give me a couple, okay?"

Thinking better of indulging in one of Sally's famous bakery items even though my sweet tooth was singing, I wiggled onto the barstool and waited. I was happy with my curves just the way they were, even though I'd recently dropped a pound or two since I took over the ranch. The physical work had toned me up in places I'd kinda forgotten I had.

Today's trip into town was mainly to pick up medicine from the vet for granddad's prized breeding mare, Maisy. The horse had scratched her right eye on something, becoming infected. Dr. Cranston's nurse had set up an early tele-health appointment this morning, and after a quick look at the horse's eye, he prescribed an antibiotic ointment and made a promise to visit the mare in the next couple of days.

With no staff since I had to let everyone go last week, this trip had me apprehensive. Not that I didn't want to take care of granddad's horse, now my horse, but because I wasn't sure how fast word had spread about the ranch's problems.

But the main reason was of a more personal nature. I'd learned through the town grapevine that the town's golden boy was back.

The boy who'd been a thorn in my side since our friendship had deteriorated once we entered high school. But thankfully after the quick stop of the vet's and then picking up groceries and stopping at the post office, I finally felt I could relax.

No one had said a word to me about the thieving manager or the Casanova Cowboy. I really hated that nickname. No doubt Lawson Bridges did as well. Although from what I remembered from the last time I'd seen him, at a kegger on graduation night with his arms around two of my fellow cheerleaders as they walked away from the bonfire, he more than earned it. Giggles had carried on the wind that night as wolf whistles followed the trio into the dark...

"Here you are, Jana. Anything else? The blueberry turnovers are hot out of the oven." Sally's words startled me. The unexpected memory had hit me hard, and I'd zoned out as I waited for my latte. Focusing on the shorter woman, I smiled my thanks.

She and I had been friendly in high school, and she'd tried to get me to join her girls' nights when I moved back to the ranch. I'd come up with every excuse I could think of, but I knew I'd have to give in soon enough. Not because I didn't like her. She was easy to like. No, I didn't go because she was *his* cousin, and I didn't want to know how the one cowboy I'd secretly wanted was living his best life, and I was cleaning up a mess I'd never seen coming.

"Sal don't tempt me. I'm still working off those chocolate croissants you sent me home with last week." I offered her a grin and took a sip of my coffee. "See you next time." I let out a long sigh. Just a few more steps, and I'd be outside.

Reaching for the diner's door handle, a large poster on the wall caught my gaze. It was of a man perched on the back of a bronc. One hand gripped tight to the saddle, his athletic body stretched, leaning back as he attempted to tame the animal between his thick thighs. My gaze traveled up the male's hard body, stopping on his tanned forearm; veins bulging. Why was that area of man's body so hot? Made me wonder if he was veiny in other hidden areas.

Whoa, where'd that thought come from? My gaze snapped to the man's sharp, high cheekbones and dimpled chin. It was the face of countless teenaged fantasies best forgotten. My body warmed as I stood unmoving, admiring the professional bronc rider.

Rattled by my body's reaction to the photo, I jumped when Sally called out to me, "He's back in town, you know. Won't talk to anyone about the accident, says he's fine. But that's Law for you. Never did like to share his troubles with anyone."

The photographer had captured Lawson's grin of pure joy laced with grit and determination as he battled against the will of the creature locked between those thighs. *Again with the thighs, Jana?*

Well, I almost made it without hearing his name. And here I was drooling over his poster that made all my girly parts perk up and take notice. It'd been sixteen years and the boy I secretly crushed on all through school was now the only man who could turn me on without touching me. And lord help me, he was back in Cedar Ridge.

CHAPTER TWO

LAWSON

Driving out to the Bennett farm with the sun high over the rolling hills, nostalgia hit me hard. The smell of fresh cut hay, memories and regrets slammed into me as I passed old man Tanner's farm. Developers had recently purchased it. Wishing progress had bypassed my hometown was like wishing for another chance at the perfect ride on the back of my favorite horse, Rocket.

Passing the shuttered schoolhouse with its peeling red paint and rusted playground equipment brought on a memory that punched me hard.

It was the first time I saw her. In that schoolyard. She tripped, and I tried to help her, but she told me she didn't need any help. In an instant, I was hooked. Jana had been a spitfire I'd wanted to tame without understanding why at seven years old. Over the years, I understood better why I found her so captivating and my feelings developed into what I thought was love, but what the hell did I know about love? My mom left when I was ten and my dad was an asshole drunk of a ranch hand.

At the end of middle school, my hormones kicked in and all my waking thoughts centered around Jana Bennett. If I were honest with myself, those hormones filled years did a number on me and set me up good.

In high school, she had me hard every time I watched her bouncing around in her short cheerleader outfit. And I knew plenty of other guys felt the same. It burned me up every time I heard her name on another guy's lips in the locker room.

When my best friend asked her to our first school dance and she said yes, I made it my mission to break them up. I was an ass because I couldn't have her.

Having spent my summers working on the Bennett farm for her grandfather, the old man caught me looking at Jana the year we turned fourteen. He'd warned me off. Said if I tried anything with her, he'd cut me loose.

Making the decision to stay away from her was the hardest thing I'd ever done, then or since. Being able to get away from my dad plus my love for riding, then competing were the two things driving me toward a better life for myself. So, I kept my true feelings to myself and pushed her away. But that didn't keep me from pining for her.

The ache for her eased some when I left for the riding circuit. Out of sight, out of mind. Or at least that's what I'd hoped. But my dreams never got that memo. Whenever I saw a woman with similar features to her or had auburn hair, my sleeping mind took over and tortured me. I often compared any woman I took to bed to her, wishing it was her.

Today I was on my way to offer my help. If I couldn't compete on the back of a horse anymore, I'd use my knowledge of horses to help her bring the Bennett Ranch back to its former standing.

And I wanted a shot at winning Jana's heart.

I pulled up to the farmhouse and let my gaze wander over the two-story structure. It could use a fresh coat of paint. The roof needed a few repairs, and the windows were coated with grime and dust. Old man Bennett had always prided himself on the upkeep of the ranch and all its buildings. To see that the illness and mismanagement of the former manager had allowed the entire operation to fall into disrepair and financial peril created a huge knot in my stomach.

Determined to convince Jana I wasn't the smart-ass boy I used to be and that I could help her, I jogged up the wooden steps onto the sagging porch. Creaks and groans sounded under my weight as I strode up to the front door and knocked. Taking in a deep breath, I said the silent prayer I used to recite right before every ride.

Long minutes passed with no response, so I stepped off the porch and checked the side of the house. Her grandpa's old Ford pickup was parked in front of the breeding barn. She had to be home. I stomped back to the front door and pounded louder.

This time, it didn't take long. She answered in nothing but a towel, water droplets streamed down her face and onto to the top of her full breasts. Eyes wild and wide, her jaw dropped open, both of us at a loss for words.

My prayer had never worked so well.

CHAPTER THREE

JANA

I had spent the afternoon wrangling Maisy, and I stank. The mare was not happy about having goop put into her eye and I had the bruises on my ass to prove it. Sweaty and dusty after finally getting enough ointment applied plus her blinders so she wouldn't rub it off or cause more damage, I took a long, hot soak in the old claw-foot tub. It was one of the few luxuries I allowed myself after a month of running the ranch on a shoestring. The last month had left me little time to indulge in anything.

Soaping up, a faint knocking made me pause. I ignored it, turning my thoughts back to the dilemma of finding a new stud for Maisy. If I was going to restore the breeding program, I needed to find someone willing to take a gamble and offer up a stud without expecting the usual upfront fee so I could then attract the riders who were willing to pay premium pricing for the offspring. Selling rights to unborn foals was a huge risk.

Every time I thought about it, it sounded crazier and more desperate. But it was the only thing short of selling the land that I could come up with that might generate enough money to pay off the bills I inherited. Big, huge emphasis on might.

But if it worked, then I could eventually hire a manager I could trust, then one day get my life back.

Loud, rapid-fire pounding rang out from the first floor. Dammit. Whoever was causing that racket better have a good reason for interrupting my bath. Grabbing a bath sheet, I wrapped it around myself and hustled downstairs, leaving small pools of water in my wake.

Opening the front door, I experienced the second shock of my life in less than a month. My mouth dropped open, my hands went slack, and I almost dropped my towel. "What are you doing here?" It was not my best moment.

Hat in hand, Lawson Bridges stood on the front porch igniting every nerve ending I possessed and a few that had been dormant so long I squeezed my thighs together and locked my knees in a vain attempt to keep from falling over.

I'd given him too much room in my brain lately and now, somehow, my thoughts had conjured him. In a daze, I noticed his eyes locked on my chest. I held the front of my towel all the tighter, praying the fabric was thick enough to hide my body's instant response to his nearness. My nipples were rock hard. Because of course they were.

"Jana." Lawson tipped his chin down in greeting. "It's good to see you again. I'm sorry for the pounding. I saw your granddad's truck and figured you were in the house."

My good sense returned as his velvety voice raised goosebumps along my exposed skin. "You, ah, caught me at a bad time. Can this wait?" With my hand on the door frame, I shifted with the intention of slamming it in his face.

"I was hoping to talk to you about the ranch, restarting the breeding operation. I'm not sure if you heard, but I'm no longer on the circuit and I've got time on my hands and…"

My gaze slammed onto said hands. Lawson's long, slim, tanned hands. His fingers fidgeted around the rim of his worn Stetson. Swallowing the sudden lump in my throat, I felt a rush of warmth bloom between my breasts. No, no, and oh, hell no. This couldn't be happening.

I hadn't seen him in years, but my body reacted as if it was just yesterday I was lusting after him in science class.

I needed to get Lawson off my porch and my ranch before I did something crazy.

So I asked him the one sure thing that would get him to leave. "I heard. Are you sure you'd be able to keep up with the physical demands of overseeing the care of my horses and the daily needs of an operation like this?" Instant regret filtered through me at my harsh tone.

The only indication I'd pissed him off was the slight flaring of his nostrils, but I knew I'd made a direct hit.

"You seem to be misinformed, Jana. My injury was to my wrist and although it's going to keep me from ever competing again, my ability to work with horses shouldn't be in doubt. Heck, I know more about running this ranch than anyone except for your grandad. And as far as my… stamina goes, well, I welcome any and all opportunities to show you I can handle anything that needs doing on the ranch, or elsewhere, for that matter." His gaze shifted from my face to my body. Was Lawson Bridges flirting with me?

I wasn't sure how to handle this side of him. It had been so long since we'd been friends that I all I remembered was the endless teasing and jokes at my expense.

"I'm gonna cut to the chase here because I know time is against you. I have a stud, or rather money, to invest in a stud. You have one mare left. Maisy, right? Let's let nature take its course. I'm not here to take advantage of the situation. I cared about your granddad. He had faith in my riding ability when no one else did. I owe him. And I think we could be a good team." Lawson again let his gaze drop to my cleavage. "C'mon, Jana. What do you have to lose?"

I let out a weird sounding snort at his question. What do I have to lose? More money? The ranch? My mind? More importantly, my heart. Because I knew at that moment I was going to say yes. Taking a chance on Lawson and this ranch might lead me to financial success, but it could also lead me to epic heartbreak if I took up his unspoken, sexy invitation.

"You've really caught me off guard. Now's not the best time and..." I stopped talking. What could I say that wouldn't sound awful or bitchy? "Sorry, I don't want your help Lawson. I'm not sure why you'd give it to someone you either ignored or teased in high school. I don't want your pity or your sympathy, Lawson."

Awkward silence hung between us. Here he was offering me a solution on a silver platter, and all I could think about was how my feelings had been hurt all those years ago when we were stupid teenagers who didn't know how to handle our emotions. Well, mine anyway.

"Why put your name on this, Lawson? We've never gotten along and even though you're no longer competing, you have a big name in the riding world. You can write your own ticket. If I agree, and that's a big if, why?"

His gaze became hooded, the color of his eyes darkened as I fidgeted, waiting for him to answer my question. What was I missing here? I'm sure he had better options than spending his time on my grandfather's rundown ranch chasing the pipe dream I created just so I could walk away one day with a clear conscious.

Instant guilt overcame me as I thought about grandad's pride in the program he nurtured and grew into one of the country's best. And guilt over becoming so caught up in my own life and not visiting or staying in touch with him as he aged so that maybe all of this could have been avoided.

"Jana? Look, I can give you more time. I don't want to rush you. But this is something I can do. I can train the horses. I'll work with the vet. I know there's an apartment over the barn where the last manager lived, so I can be on site twenty-four seven. Plus, I saved as much of my prize money as I could and still have a comfortable life while on the circuit. At my age, if the injury hadn't ended my career, then time would. So, I've got some money to invest and a passion for horses. For me, this is a win-win. Your grandfather gave me so much when I was a kid, nurtured my dream. Let me help."

Lawson was the answer to every prayer I'd sent up since returning to the ranch. If that wasn't the universe telling me to take a chance, then, well, I didn't deserve the opportunity. And I would be a fool to ignore it and him.

"This isn't a quick or fast fix, Law. Are you absolutely sure you want to make this type of time commitment?"

He remained silent. His intense gaze making me squirm again. I felt like an awkward teenager all of a sudden. It reminded me of all the times we were at the same parties, ignoring each other. Pretending we didn't care who the other was dating. At least that was the way it was for me.

"The way I see it, you need help or you're going to have to sell. Accept my help, Jana. Whether you like it or not, I feel as invested in this ranch as you. Cedar Ridge deserves this chance to keep the untamed development from altering our way of life."

I wanted more than anything to accept his help. But my

reaction to him kicked off major warning bells. This would be asking for heartbreak if I had to see him day after day. And I wasn't interested in revisiting that time when I pined for Lawson to notice me or find out why he walked away from our friendship. Could I honestly handle seeing him, being around him every day and not let my long-buried feelings for him bubble back up?

"How about you come back to tomorrow? I need to sleep on it. And I need to be dressed the next time we see each other."

He put his hat back on, nodded his head and flashed me a wide grin. Before I could get the door closed, his gaze zeroed in on my face. It's intensity lighting me up.

"What you're wearing now suits me fine, but I'll be back after breakfast. I promise you won't regret it, Jana."

I closed the door firmly, then collapsed backward onto the hard wood. I felt my face flush at Lawson's teasing words.

I already knew my answer. Please don't let me regret this grandad.

CHAPTER FOUR

LAWSON

I was up before dawn thinking about Jana. And that towel wrapped around her curves. She had no way of knowing what she did to me. During our entire conversation, it was all I could do to keep my cock from announcing its presence. Damn, she was more beautiful now than in school.

I wish I could have been here sooner and been able to attend Mr. Bennett's funeral. But I had just gone through surgery when I heard the news, then I needed to go through a round of intense physical therapy to regain the use of my left hand.

Smiling at the memory of her questioning my stamina, I threw off the bed sheets and headed for the shower. My plan was to head over to the Sunrise Diner and pick up some of my cousin Sally's fancy pastries and a couple of coffees to go, then be back at Jana's place before she ate her breakfast. I wasn't so proud that I wouldn't use my cousin's cinnamon rolls to help me in my cause.

For the second time in two days, I found myself driving out to the Bennett Ranch. When I was there yesterday, I couldn't help but notice how quiet things were. The corral was empty. No sounds rang out from the bunkhouse.

Damn, I wish I could get my hands on that manager that screwed old man Bennett and Jana over. I'd heard that she hadn't been back to the place in years. She'd been living up in Pineville working at a law firm. I knew this ranch hadn't been her dream, but here she was, determined to save it.

Now I just had to convince her I was the man to help her. And maybe I could test the waters, see if what I felt pass between us yesterday had been real. Because if there was one woman I could see myself growing old with, it was Jana Bennett.

She still wore her dark auburn hair long and my fingers itched to grab a handful and tug her close so I could kiss her senseless. And her hazel eyes were just as expressive as when I teased her endlessly in high school. I never didn't regret that. I loved seeing her get all riled up. But I do regret never telling her how I really felt, how I listened to her granddad and stayed away until I was eighteen. And then I wasn't quick enough after because she took off for college and I hit the circuit.

I hope I didn't mess up this second chance at making things right with her.

I parked my truck next to hers, grabbed the coffee and breakfast treats, and practiced my speech as I walked back up the porch. The door swung open before I had a chance to knock.

"You're earlier than I expected." Jana, fully dressed, crossed her arms over her chest. Her expression was both wary and welcoming. Finding myself tongue tied, I took in her curves as she pivoted toward the kitchen. Gifted with a view of her perfect heart-shaped ass I couldn't hold back a grin. I found myself thinking about how I could get my hands on her. And soon.

Placing the coffee on the table, I held up the bag and shook it slightly. "Fresh, hot and guaranteed to make you happy and satisfied until lunchtime."

Jana fisted her hands on her hips. "Lawson Bridges, don't tell me you have cinnamon rolls in that bag."

"Okay, I won't." I opened the bag and dug in.

"Give me that. Lord, I love Sally's frosting." Jana grabbed the bag and held it to her chest, then opened it and took in a deep breath.

My cock twitched, and I froze at the ecstasy on her face. Trouble with a capital T stood in front of me and all I could do was imagine licking frosting off her full breasts.

"Lawson?"

I snapped out of my lust induced haze, barely, when she said my name. "Um, yeah?"

A small smile spread across her face. "This is so nice of you. I know the competition is fierce at the diner first thing in the morning. Thank you." She turned around, took a couple of plates down, and joined me at the table.

I watched as she nibbled on a few pieces of the pastry. It was torture. "Jana, go for it. No judgement." I grabbed mine, taking a large bite, then licked my fingers clean.

Her cheeks flushed prettily as she watched me. Between large sips of coffee and polishing off our cinnamon rolls for the first time in a long time, heck maybe the actual first time, I felt comfortable with a woman. Oh, I was still worked up for Jana, but there was something more going on here.

In the past, it was simply about finding someone to hook up with before the night ended. In this moment it was about two old friends, at least I was hoping we could be friends again. If she agreed to let me help, then maybe by spending time together, working together to save the ranch, something more could develop between us.

Man, she was so pretty sitting there, the morning light streaming in through the kitchen window highlighting her burnished auburn hair. "Okay, so have you given thought to my proposal?"

She cleaned up our dishes and stood in front of the farm sink, staring off into the distance. I couldn't take my eyes off her. Things seemed to be moving fast, but I knew the last sixteen years had been building up to this moment when I could come back home and win over the girl of my dreams.

I'd never been more nervous than I was right now. "If you need to see a financial statement, I've got paperwork in my truck. And you know how I am with horses after all the years I worked on the ranch and training with your granddad. Tell me what you need to keep the ranch?"

She turned to face me, crossing her arms. "I'm not going to lie to you, Lawson. The situation is about as bad as it can get. I've been able to make good on all the outstanding debts except for a fifty-thousand-dollar balloon payment due in three months and one contract for an as yet conceived foal.

I had to sell off all the horses except for Maisy to cover all the unpaid feed and vet bills plus cover the outstanding wages for the ranch hands and granddad's housekeeper the manager had siphoned before he took off. If you really want to help me, then we need to agree on a few things first."

Word hadn't spread about the balloon payment. He could cover that easily. But would she let him in exchange for part ownership of the ranch? He wasn't even sure she wanted to keep the ranch once she paid off the bills, plus the contract for the next foal from Maisy that had already been paid for.

"If they're reasonable, I'm sure there won't be any issues. Shoot. I'm all ears." He offered her a reassuring smile and waited.

"Okay, first, I'm in charge. I intend to see the ranch restored to what it was before he got sick. If an interested buyer shows up, they'll have to sign a piece of paper stating they'll continue the operation for at least twenty years. I'm no fool. I know the odds are against me as a single woman running a ranch with little experience except being raised on it till I was eighteen. But I'm not going to let someone buy this land just to turn it into a bunch of cookie-cutter houses. Second, with you here, and if you agree to help, I can begin advertising for boarding services again. With the money I make from that, I can hire a couple of local teens to work part time. Then down the road, if the profit margin is good, I'll invest in a few horses strictly for riding lessons and after that, add trail riding horses for rent."

I nodded. Sounded perfectly reasonable. She'd obviously put a lot of thought into things, and she knew she couldn't do this all on her own.

Jana let out a big breath and continued. "I'd like our agreement in writing for the stud services and the hours you'll be putting in on the ranch. Depending on how long it takes to...I mean, for, uh, nature to take its course, I don't have a problem with you living in the apartment above the barn. But no women, Lawson. You want to scratch an itch, you do it somewhere else."

I didn't bat an eye. As far as I was concerned, she was the only one I'd be scratching anything with.

Her cheeks turned pink on her last statement, but with her chin tilted slightly up, it was as if she was daring me to argue.

"No problem. When can I move in?"

CHAPTER FIVE

JANA

Two weeks had passed since Lawson showed up with coffee and cinnamon rolls and upended my life. From the delivery of the stud he'd purchased to handling everything with the vet to making sure Sir Chancellor and Maisy were set up to mate, Lawson seemed to be in his element. He knew so much more about horses and all I knew was how to ride one, and I hadn't done that in years. He hadn't asked for a stake in the ranch. Just wanted to payback what he felt granddad had given him in mentorship.

There weren't many men like Lawson in this world, at least not that she'd met. He was making it awfully hard not to fall for him all over again.

I handled all the paperwork and accounting items, even though it wasn't my favorite thing. I'd called Kelee a couple times for her help. She told me she wanted to visit, but I kept putting her off. I wasn't ready to combine my old life with the new. Maybe once Maisy was pregnant, I could relax a bit.

Archer King, the developer who offered to the buy the ranch shortly after granddad died, still wasn't taking no for an answer. In his last voicemail, he said he had a new venture he wanted to discuss with me and would I be willing to meet him for dinner the next time he was in the area.

I hadn't said anything to Lawson about the messages. I didn't want to give him any reason to think I wasn't all in on our plan. Well, mostly my plan. He seemed happy dealing with the horses while I handled everything else.

Seeing him every day allowed me an insight into the real man, not the Cowboy Casanova label he'd been tagged with so many years ago. I saw a side to him I wouldn't have if he hadn't offered to help.

Besides being handsome and making me hot and bothered any time we were together, he was kind, funny and nothing like the smartass teen I remembered.

Except for the flirting he'd done those first couple of days, the only indication I got that he saw me as a woman and not a friend was when I'd catch him looking at me. I felt the burn of those heated glances to my bones. But when I caught him looking, he'd put his friendly mask back in place.

But I had a feeling I knew what he was thinking because I was thinking the same thing. And I was thinking more and more about scratching the constant itch his presence was creating within me.

The alarm I'd set on my watch dinged at a quarter past four. I'd been working in the former manager's office, mine now, spending more time thinking about how nice Lawson's ass looked in his jeans than on the website I was trying to update. Sighing, I closed up the office and headed to the house to get showered and changed.

I'd finally agreed to see Archer and hear him out, if only to stop his phone calls. On my way out, I heard a strange noise coming from the stalls. Maisy and Sir Chancellor had gotten busy a few days ago, and Lawson was keeping close tabs on her until he could do a pregnancy test.

Making my way down the long aisle toward the mare's stall, my gaze landed on the backside I had been dreaming about moments ago. Lawson was feeding the mare carrots her, rubbing her neck and talking in low, sweet tones to her.

"Is that how you got all the girls to chase after you?" Realizing that my voice sounded a bit breathy, maybe even seductive, I hid turned my face away so he couldn't read my thoughts. How he made me feel all tingly inside whenever we were close. Or how the need he created within me made me want to throw all caution to the wind by pressing myself up against him and beg him to take me.

Why was it so difficult for me to just let go and tell him how I felt, what I wanted? One thing I'd never had a problem with before he came back into my life was letting men know what I wanted from them. A good time, nothing more.

But with Lawson, a part of me knew a good time meant more than having his hands on me because it wouldn't be enough.

CHAPTER SIX

LAWSON

I finished up in the barn thinking I'd ask Jana if she wanted to grab something to eat at the diner when a late model luxury SUV pulled up to the ranch house. Jana stepped out the front door and sent him a wave and a bright smile. What was going on?

Jealousy flamed within me as the man got way too close to Jana. It was a feeling I'd never felt about a woman before and it was throwing me way out of my comfort zone. Although what I was feeling for Jana was no game. She wasn't someone I wanted just one night with. I wanted more and seeing this guy in a suit sweet-talking her kicked into high gear every protective instinct I had.

"Jana, who's this? You going to introduce me?" I couldn't help it. I stepped in between them. Maybe not the best way to handle the situation, but seeing this guy next to her made my blood boil.

"Excuse me, Archer. I'll be right back."

Jana pulled me back toward the house. Her grip on my forearm ignited much more than the protective rush of adrenaline. It flooded my senses, the need for her to be mine and no one else's.

"He's here to talk, Lawson. Please don't get into a pissing match with him. I'm curious what his plans are and if I can't make the balloon payment, I think it's smart to have a backup plan, don't you?"

Not if it meant seeing her leave with another man took her to dinner dressed like that, it didn't. But he couldn't say that to her. He didn't have any rights to her. Yet.

If anyone was going to take Jana to bed, it would be him.

"What are you thinking? It's only been a couple of weeks; you need to give this a chance. What happened to 'I won't let this land turn into track housing?' Don't you have any allegiance to your granddad's legacy?" *Dammit.* I wanted to take back the words as soon as they left my mouth.

Jana reared back as if I'd hit her.

"Whoa. Where do you get off speaking to me like that?" Jana's face flushed red.

I paced the length of the porch. It didn't get me very far. Or far enough from her. I was desperate to get my hands on her. *Make her stay and listen to reason.* But I knew that would only cause further problems between us.

"I'm sorry. You're right." Taking another deep breath, I stopped pacing. "Where's he taking you? Can I at least ask that? Just so I know, in case of an emergency or something." I was reaching, and I knew it.

Jana shook her head. Confusion filling her face. "I accept your apology. Please don't worry. I'm a grown woman, Lawson. I can handle him if he tries anything." She waited a beat until I nodded at her. "It's just dinner. I should be back long before dark."

Not trusting myself to keep from saying something stupid to him like "keep your hands off my woman" I leaned against the porch railing and crossed my feet hoping she'd take it as a peace offering when it was anything but. Seeing her dressed in that killer outfit for dinner with another man ate me up inside. I didn't know if I could hold back my growing feelings for her any longer. She may already know I wanted her body, but what she had no idea of was how I wanted to hide her away all to myself—forever.

Admitting it to myself should have thrown me into a major internal freak-out. I'd spent years avoiding anything serious with women. Hell, it was so easy to do with my lifestyle, the career I'd chosen. But something had always held me back from seeking out anything permanent. And now I knew what. Or rather, who.

Jana. It had always been Jana for me.

I nodded at her statement and watched as she spun around to rejoin Archer and, like a damn puppy; I turned and watched her. I felt a gut punch when the developer glanced at me. A quick smirk appeared on his too handsome face. It took everything in me to keep from following her to his car and doing something idiotic.

Their words filtered back toward me as I stewed over someone else spending time with Jana. Why couldn't I just admit to her what was in my heart? And if I didn't make a move to let her know soon, either this guy or someone else was going to lock her down because women like Jana were few and far between. I was just lucky she hadn't found someone before now.

I needed a plan to win her over without playing the

jealous he-man, which I'd never been, but there was something about Jana that was bringing it out in me.

CHAPTER SEVEN

JANA

The restaurant had been nice, the conversation nice, the reasoning for selling the ranch sounded sensible. However, as I sat across from Archer, all I found myself doing was comparing him to Lawson.

Both men were handsome. But that's where the similarities ended. I didn't have to hide my body's reaction when I was with Archer, because there wasn't one. Although in another universe I might be attracted to him, he didn't do anything for me physically. He didn't have work-hardened hands, sinewy muscles, or Lawson's sarcastic humor.

I spent the drive back to the ranch, silently comparing the two men. And the more I did, I realized maybe Archer would be a good match for Kelee if she lived here. Something to think about as I considered her many requests to come visit and help me. I knew she was looking for a change, but until I was sure my plan was really going to work, I didn't want to get her hopes up.

"Thanks for hearing me out tonight, Jana. Whether you decide to sell off part of the ranch or all of it, I want to be the first person you call." Archer parked the black Escalade behind my granddad's beat up twenty-five-year-old pickup and angled his body toward me.

Was he going to try and kiss me? I saw a brief flash of interest in his gaze at dinner, but he hadn't given off any signals that he was interested in pursuing something beyond business with me. How could I tactfully avoid his interest without letting it affect a possible business deal if and when I needed it?

Instead of leaning into me, Archer grinned and pointed to something behind me. "Looks like your partner's been waiting up for you."

Confused, I looked out the passenger door window. Lawson was striding toward the SUV with a scowl on his face. What in the world was he up to?

"I'll say goodnight and offer one last pitch. If you decide to sell to me, please remember I want to respect the integrity of what your grandfather built here and his love for the land. All plots in our development will be no less than five acres. Seeing the beauty of this area and getting to know the citizens of Cedar Ridge, I don't want urban sprawl ruining this part of the state any more than you do."

I managed to tear my gaze from Lawson when he'd stopped feet away from the vehicle. Arms crossed and his head held high, his eyes were laser focused on the door I was sitting behind. With the dark tinted windows, could he see inside?

"I appreciate that Archer. And if things don't go as we planned with restarting the breeding program, you'll be hearing from me. Thank you again for dinner." I took a deep breath before facing whatever was going on in Lawson's head and opened the door.

"Goodnight. And good luck."

Chuckling followed me out of the car. I stood still, watching the vehicle disappear down the long drive away from the barn until its taillights faded. Only then did I turn to face Lawson. I felt waves of heat coming from him as I stepped closer to him.

"Do you know what time it is? I've been trying to reach you." Censor lacing his voice, Law dropped his arms and fisted his hands onto his hips.

"Sorry, Dad. Didn't know I had a curfew." Was that jealousy I heard in his tone, or had he reverted to the asshole he'd once been? Either way, he had no say in how I spent my time.

His body jerked at my words, and I froze. We were now less than a foot apart. Something dark had entered his eyes. Not sure if I wanted to find out why he was so worked up, I stepped toward the house, away from a Lawson I'd never seen before.

"Sweetheart, comparing me to your father is not something you want to do right now. Rest assured, what I'm feeling right now is the furthest thing from fatherly as I can get. But I'll table that for now. Maisy's been off all evening and—"

Maisy? Worry hit me hard at the thought something had happened to the prized mare. I'd tried so hard not to become attached to her, and oh, lord, I wasn't here when she needed me. I ran toward the barn, stumbling, then quickly recovering as I ran through the open doors toward her stall.

He was following so close to me, his heat and scent encompassed me, creating tiny shivers all over my body.

"Jana, stop. You're going to twist an ankle in those damn heels."

I didn't care. I just needed to see her for myself. "What's wrong with her?"

"Nothing. She's fine."

We were both out of breath by the time I made it to her stall. I reached up and stroked her nose as she angled her head over the gate. Whispering softly, my gaze raked over the mare's flanks, down her legs. She appeared to be fine. But maybe. Oh, what if she had a miscarriage? The thought chilled me. So much was riding on Maisy getting pregnant after the first breeding attempt. It wasn't unusual for a second attempt to be required, but the thought of her going through something like that and without me cut deep.

"Okay, she's fine. Then what had you so worried about her that had you acting all alpha-hole when I got home?"

"Alpha-hole? Listen, I had a real concern. She was down longer than I'd ever seen her, so I called the vet. He left about thirty minutes ago. She got back up shortly before he arrived. The doc checked her over, said she was fine." He ran a hand along her neck and gave her a couple pats. The horse whinnied at the attention.

Lawson was standing at my back, so close that if I took in a deep breath, our bodies would touch. My body instantly relaxed at the news she was okay, but my anger at his behavior continued to simmer. I needed to understand what was going on between us. I either needed his hands on me or to push him away for good. This constant dancing around each other had to stop.

I looked at his strong profile and sighed. "Well, you couldn't see how you looked. I don't appreciate you treating me as if I was doing something wrong, Lawson. We don't have that type of relationship."

A long stretch of silence passed between us. Too long. I turned until I was fully facing him. It was now or never. "I'm tired of pretending, Lawson. I'm in a constant state of need whenever you're near me. We're not kids anymore and if I don't tell you now, then I never will."

"Tell me." Lawson's husky timbre encouraged me, heated me inside and out.

"I want you, Law." I raised my hands and cradled his face, his five o'clock shadow scratching my fingers, sending tiny shocks from the tips of my fingers and down my arms. "Now. I want you." Raising up on my toes, I pressed my lips against his, feathering light kisses along his full mouth. Before I could deepen the kiss, he grabbed me around the waist, pulling me in tight against him. His erection pressed into my belly, his full-throated moan against my mouth, leaving no doubt he wanted the same thing.

The kiss was wild and full of the type of passion I'd only dreamed of. Lifting me into his arms, he spun around and stepped into the empty stall next to Maisy's, pressing me up against the wood siding, his hands running through my hair as he kissed my jaw, my neck, and the top of my breasts.

"Hell, I've been half hard for you night and day, Jana. I don't think I can make it to a bed."

With shaking hands, I pushed him back a step so I could unbutton my dress. I watched him as his gaze followed my every move as I let the material drop and stood there in my bra and panties. He mumbled incoherently, running his hand over his mouth as I peeled my bra straps down and flung it over his shoulder. When I went to kick off my heels, he stopped me.

"Leave 'em." His words thrilled me as he made quick

work of his shirt, then his buckle, and pants joined my clothes tossed onto the hay strewn dirt floor of the stall.

I didn't care where we were, I just needed him.

Lawson cupped the underside of my breasts and dipped his head, taking a hard nipple into his hot mouth. He sucked and swirled his tongue around the tip while his left thumb teased its twin. A rush of warmth from his touch had me rubbing them together. I needed him closer. I rocked my hips, searching for him.

In a move leaving me dizzy, he spun me around and put my arms over my head and onto the wood siding.

"Don't move. Let me do all the work. I just want to hear you scream my name when you come."

His hands were everywhere. My breasts, my hips, and the curve of my ass. He pulled me into his hard erection, rubbing himself against me while at the same time he dipped his hand between my thighs and thrust two fingers between my slick folds. I heard a moan that I didn't recognize as my own until his mouth found my ear and whispered, "Damn, you're so responsive. And wet. Just for me."

I couldn't speak as his fingers played with my clit, then stroked me deep. The pressure from his body behind me, and his fingers inside of me, had me chasing my orgasm. I rocked my hips, searching for my release.

"Not yet. I need to taste you. Want you to come on my mouth." Lawson pulled his hands away then spun me round. Kneeling in front of me, he caught my gaze and grinned. "Damn, you're gorgeous. Hair mussed from my hands, pussy wet from my touch. Just lean back, baby."

Dazed, I did what he wanted. What I wanted.

His mouth devoured me. Tongue diving deep, then flicking my clit. I could feel my orgasm building. Impatient,

I ground myself down and rode the first crest as it broke, my entire being exploding into tiny electric shocks when he pressed his thumb on my clit while still fucking me with his tongue. "Lawson...yes!" I screamed his name again as he continued milking my orgasm until I slumped back, my thighs shaking and threatening to give out.

"I got you, darlin'." Lawson stood, wrapped one hand around my waist and gripped his cock in the other. "Tell me this is what you want, Jana." He buried his head in neck. "I don't have a condom on me. I'll stop if you want me to, but tell me now."

Need and desperation filled his voice. He would do exactly that if I asked him too, but I wanted him more than my next breath. "I...I'm good. We're good. I just had my period a few days ago. I want this. I want you inside me. Now."

Lawson filled me, stretched me, then lifted me under my ass. He braced his hand against the wall behind me. "Lean forward onto me. I don't want your back to get scratched up."

"But your wrist. I don't want you to re-injure it." He'd been wearing a brace since he showed up on the ranch to help keep it in place while it healed.

"That's the last thing I'm worried about. Now hold on." He captured my lips, held me in one hand, and slid into me.

Slowly, over and over, he thrust into me, driving me higher. But I didn't want slow and gentle.

I rocked my hips against him, ramping up my pace. "Lawson." Responding to my plea, he began to thrust faster, stroking me deeper. My inner walls grasped around his cock when another orgasm rushed through me.

Screaming his name over and over, my body vibrating

when he changed his angle ever so slightly and found my g-spot. "Right there, yes!" Another wave hit me and we came together as our sweat slicked bodies slapped against each other, the sound echoing around the stall. The smell of hay, earth and our mingling scents would live with me forever.

CHAPTER EIGHT

JANA

I woke up the next morning in Lawson's bed alone. My first thought was, *'What was I thinking?'* Having unprotected sex with Lawson was not anywhere on my to do list in getting the ranch back up and running. Having sex with Lawson without discussing our feelings for each wasn't on it either.

But was I sorry?

No way.

There's way no way I'd regret the experience. One that ruined me for anyone else. Period. But did he feel the same way?

The smell of coffee had me sitting up and searching for something to put on. Our clothes had not made the journey from the stall to Lawson's room. I found one of his flannel shirts in a laundry basket and quickly buttoned it up. It fell to just above my knees. It would have to do. Coffee was calling me.

The kitchen in the apartment was fairly small. Just enough room for a refrigerator, stove, and sink, plus a few cupboards, and a counter completed the u-shaped room. Two barstools were tucked under the counter. I pulled one out and watched him cook. He'd pulled on a pair of well-worn Wranglers and nothing else. His broad muscular back bunched as he moved and I became mesmerized by the sight. His hair still mussed from my fingers and I noted faint scratch marks leading outward from his spine and along his lower back.

I felt myself flush at the evidence of my reaction to him. We'd made love again after he carried me upstairs. This time, he used a condom. But I wouldn't dwell or feel regret for the first time we had sex. It was beyond anything I'd experienced. It was perfect.

He poured me a cup of coffee, placed it in front of me, then kissed me senseless. Wrapping his hands around my arms, he hauled me up into him. "Mm. I could get used to this." He dropped a kiss on my nose, then went back to the stove. "How do you like your eggs?"

And just like that, my belly flip-flopped, my heart swelled, and there was no turning back. The teenage lust and feelings I'd had for him had morphed into something much more solid. Love. This is what love felt like. I was sure of it. Although maybe it had happened that first day he showed up on my porch, but in this moment I was able to name it.

I let it roll around in my brain as I watched him fix my breakfast while also admiring how much I liked his butt in those jeans.

"Here you go." He set the plate of scrambled eggs and bacon in front of me, then snapped his fingers. "I almost forgot. Last night when we were talking about Maisy..."

I took a bite and nodded. "Yes, and these are really good, by the way, thanks." I'm not sure if a man had ever cooked for me before. The last boyfriend I had, well, we never lived together, and I always stayed at his place, then left after a quick cup of coffee. So yeah, Lawson was giving me another first.

"Yeah, well, she's pregnant." He flashed a huge smile.

The fork fell out of my hand and I began choking on my food. Lawson patted my back until I shooed him away. "Preg—pregnant? What? You couldn't have told me last night?"

He didn't look the least bit chastened. In fact, his brows narrowed and his lips thinned out.

"I seem to recall we both had something else on our minds. Maybe like swallowing each other whole. Besides, I told you she was fine, and that's all that matters, right?" He took a deep drink of his coffee, then leaned his elbow on the counter, laced his fingers, looking sexy and relaxed.

His movements made me forget for a second why I was mad. His chest and abs were sculpted from years of riding, and needing to stay in shape for the intensity of the job. All I wanted to do was lean forward and lick him. *Wait. No. Just no.* "You're not getting off that easy, Bridges." I stood and tried to wiggle past him.

He circled his arms around me, pulling me in close. "Darlin', where do you think you're going?"

"To my house." The wind left my sails as I said the words. I didn't want to go anywhere, but the hurt I felt was real and I needed him to understand that holding information back about my horse and the future of the ranch wasn't going to cut it. His arms were like steel bands around me, and he wouldn't budge when I tried to move away.

"You can't keep that type of information from me,

Lawson. Maisy being pregnant means I can follow through on the contract to the buyer. It's the only reason I stayed and decided to put my crazy plan of saving the ranch into play. This is my future, not yours. You just took pity on me and offered me a solution."

He didn't say anything to my outburst. Instead, he loosened his hold and let out a heavy sigh. "I'm not going to keep you here if you don't want to stay. You have every right to be mad. But Jana, before you go, you need to know how special last night was to me. How important you've always been to me. And being able to help you out, make sure this ranch had a chance at continuing. Both are more than I deserve, but I just wanted you so damn much. I always have."

Lawson's eyes held so much emotion it was breaking me in two. Getting upset was one thing, but ruining a chance for something more between us was just stupid. Did I dare hope he wanted more than a night between my thighs? "Wait, what do you mean, 'always have?'"

He picked me up and carried me over to the couch and settled me on his lap. I sat ramrod straight, hands twisted in my lap, and waited.

"This has been a long time coming. Us. I'm pretty sure fell in love with you that day on the playground when you refused my offer of help. You remember that day?"

I nodded, memories overwhelming me.

"From that day until middle school, I followed you like a puppy. Then, the summer before high school, I took a break from doing the chores your granddad assigned me before he'd let me practice. I saw you riding one of the trail horses and I was lost in teenage lust, and then who finds me drooling over you? Your grandfather."

My hand flew to my mouth. I choked back tears. I couldn't believe what I was hearing.

"He lit into me and made it crystal clear that I was to keep away from you. If I so much as touched you, he was yanking my riding privileges. He scared me shitless, Jana. My mom was gone, my dad was never home and when he was all he did was yell at me. The words 'you'll never be good enough for the circuit boy' rang in my head non-stop. I had to choose my future, even if all I wanted right then was you. I had to hide my true feelings for you and make something of myself before I could ever hope of being your man."

Being shocked to my core seemed to be the theme of my life lately. First granddad passing, then Lawson showing up, and now he's declaring he wanted me all those years ago. Still wants me. "It's been, what, sixteen years, Lawson? Why should I believe you now? You've had plenty of time to come back and tell me how you really felt. Why you pushed me away and teased me endlessly through high school."

He picked up one of my hands and squeezed. "I'm sorry, baby. I figured if I kept you pissed off enough, then there wouldn't be any chance I'd slip up and tell you how I really felt. I was young and didn't have the support I needed to accomplish my dreams any other way than with your granddad's help. I need you to forgive me. Please?"

Forgiveness was easy. Forgetting was a whole other thing. I swallowed hard as a fresh wave of tears threatened to spill. Lawson pulled my hand to his lips and kissed my palm, then placed it on the side of his face, drawing my gaze to his.

His eyes were clear, bright and I could read the honesty in them. And I saw something else as he looked at me. Love.

The kind of love I so desperately wanted from him as a naïve teenager who had no clue what he was going through.

The kind of love I needed, craved as a woman.

My emotions were all over the damn place. Lawson's loving gaze was showing me what I could have if only I was willing to take a chance and let go of the iron band I'd wrapped around my heart the last time it was broken—by him.

"Let me in, Jana. Let me make up for all the time lost and create a life here with you. I think we make a pretty great team. And you can't deny the sex is spectacular. C'mon, darlin'. Let me love you for the rest of my life."

The tears finally fell. My whole body began to shake, and I threw my arms around his neck and bawled. Lawson rubbed small circles on my back, soothing me till I calmed.

"I'm such a mess. Oh, my lord, my eyes are probably puffy and red and I'm sure I've got snot hanging out of my nose." I wiped my hands over my face and found him chuckling at me.

"What? I'm right, right?"

"Darlin', you are beautiful, snot or no snot. And as if you can't tell, I've been rock hard this whole time. So maybe you could put me out of my misery and let me know. Am I forgiven?"

Oh, yes, I was well aware how his body was reacting to our closeness and I was so wet and achy all I had to do was shift slightly, straddle his lap, and sink myself onto him. In fact, that's exactly what I should do.

Grinning at him, I whipped off my shirt, his shirt, climbed over his lap, undid his zipper, and took his hard cock in hand and sank down onto his cock.

"Lawson?"

He let out garbled, "oh, yeah." His hands went to my

hips, his head fell back. I wanted this moment to last forever as I watched his face morph into pleasure. "I forgive you."

"Thank *fuuuck*. Now move."

"Uh-uh. It's your turn. Tell me what I want to hear." I smiled. Yes, this had all happened quickly, but after spending a decade and a half without him, I couldn't have asked for a better ending and new beginning.

Lawson tipped his chin down and held my watery gaze. "I love you, Jana."

A surge of joy filled me at his words and our connection.

"I love you, my Casanova Cowboy."

Our laughter faded as our need for each other took over.

EPILOGUE

JANA

Two months later

On the same day we made the balloon payment, standing in front of the justice of the peace, we made a promise to love each other through the good, the bad and everything in between. My parents flew in from Florida, Lawson's dad was there too. Pride and tears warred with each other at the reception as he raised a glass, wishing us everything he never had.

That day, a small but mighty group of supporters, friends, and family surrounded us. And today was our one-month anniversary. I never thought I'd be so sentimental, but I had a surprise for my husband. We had two more buyers bidding on Maisy's next foal with Sir Chancellor. Step by step, we'd make this operation one of the best again and we'd do it together.

Kelee had been my maid of honor and had fallen in love with Cedar Ridge. With her head for numbers and a desire for a change of pace, she offered to take over the accounting duties for Bennett-Bridges Breeding, aka the Triple B. She found a cute rental in town and had turned in her little red coupe for a used pickup.

My bestie had gone country and having her close thrilled me. Maybe she'd find a cowboy of her own soon. Then we could raise our babies together as we rebuilt the breeding operation.

Lawson had wanted to keep the original name, and I loved how sweet he was about it, but with the new name, not only were we honoring my granddad, but making his own contribution as important to the history of the ranch and its future. Lawson had built a well-earned reputation in the world of bronc riding, and that meant something to our customers.

I finished getting dressed for the dinner I had planned for Lawson and headed downstairs to the kitchen to set up the table and put his favorite casserole in the oven. My cell chimed with Kelee's tone.

KELEE: What's the name of that developer who wanted to buy the ranch a few months back?

ME: Archer King

KELEE: Dammit, thanks.

ME: Hey, don't leave me hanging. What's up?

KELEE: No worries, just ran into him at the diner. Nothing I can't handle. Besides, you've got a big night planned. Hugs!

Hm. Interesting. Wonder what brought Archer back to town? I needed to follow up with her tomorrow on how she handled the sexy developer.

"Well, what's all this?" Lawson stepped into the kitchen, a bit dusty smelling of hay, and his own unique scent.

I set down my phone and gave him a big smile. "Oh, just your favorite—Southern Fried Chicken, sweet potatoes and corn bread. Go clean up and it'll be finished when you're ready."

Lawson gave me the side-eye then looked me up and down, leaving a trail of goosebumps everywhere his gaze touched. Would I always react this way? Lord, I hoped so.

"How about you tell me what you're up to? You've been avoiding me all day and now you fixed me my favorite dinner." He closed the distance between us and rested his hands on my hips.

"Well, it's our one-month anniversary. Surprise!" I threw out a hand toward the table. "I just felt like marking the occasion."

His eyes darkened at my words. "I can think of a better way to celebrate." He bent and scooped his hands under my ass, picking me up and crushing me to his hard rock chest.

I let out a squeal as he pivoted toward the stairs. "Wait, the oven. The corn bread will burn."

He backed up and hit the button on the stove, turning it off. Grinning, he captured my lips and kissed me till we were both gasping for air. "Hold on."

Laughing, he pounded up the stairs, crossed the threshold to our room, and released me onto the bed. I bounced, my hair flying into my face, and when I swept it away, I found my husband's hot gaze locked on me as he unbuttoned his shirt, then pulled off his boots. His hand rested on his belt, then paused.

"I can't wait. I'm sorry I ruined your plans, but I need to

be inside you. Now take that pretty dress off, darlin'. Nice and slow." He finished undoing his belt, unzipped his wranglers, and pushed them off. His erection straining against his boxer briefs.

My mouth watered at the sight of him. All mine. For now. I'd be sharing him soon with the child we created that night in the barn, and I couldn't wait any longer to tell him. Maisy wasn't the only one expecting.

I crossed my arms and lifted the dress over my head, undid my bra and tossed it to the floor. Lawson followed my movements, his gaze roaming over my exposed flesh, igniting zaps of electricity everywhere. I wiggled out of my panties, then reached for him.

He bent over me, spread my legs open and settled on his knees. His warm hands skimmed along my thighs, onto my hips, up my sides, cupping my breasts. He circled his thumbs over my nipples, wrenching a moan, then a gasp from me as he pinched, then soothed the hard peaks.

"Tell me." His deep, raspy voice commanded.

"Tell you what?" My eyelids fluttered at the delicious torture his hands continued to provide.

Lawson placed a soft kiss on my lips before he placed his forehead on mine, laying down next to me. His right hand traveled south before palming my stomach.

Of course, he knew. This man had spent the last few months worshipping and learning every inch of my body. My breasts were a bit larger, and I'd been sleepier than usual. He missed nothing.

"When?" He traced circles around my belly button, wrenching another moan from me.

"Six months. Give or take. You happy? I mean, sure, we talked about kids, but not so soon—"

Lawson claimed my mouth and consumed me. His

hand dipped between my thighs, then flicked his fingers between my drenched folds.

"I'm beyond happy. Only one thing, though. No telling junior he got his start in the breeding barn."

I busted out laughing and crying at the same time, then nodded. For this man, I'd agree to just about anything.

WORTH THE WAIT

Two wounded souls discover an unexpected connection.

Cole

I lost more than my lower left leg just a month before my last tour was scheduled to end. I lost three of my men.

Two years later, I've accepted and overcome my physical wounds, but my mental health still needs some work. I come back home to Pineville to see my sister and face the demons that pushed me away fifteen years ago.

What I didn't plan on finding was the curvy single mom next door stirring up equal parts naughty nighttime, heck *anytime* thoughts and unfamiliar feelings—feelings I never thought were in the cards for me. Then there's a determined five-year-old looking to scale the oak tree in my backyard while working his way into my heart.

Can I let either into my life while I'm still trying to come to terms with my past?

Scarlett

I'm determined to finish my MBA six years after dropping out of college. I'll do most anything to ensure a better life for my son. And if that means working two jobs, living with my grandmother—who helps take care of my son—and giving up any time for myself, so be it. It's not like I'm looking for another guy who thinks he knows what's best for me. So, I need to be careful who I let into my bed and my heart because my priorities are my son, work and getting that degree.

Which means I don't have time for the sometimes grumpy, always protective, and oh-so-sexy, wounded hero next door who becomes my temporary chauffeur, plays catch with my son, and makes me burn with a simple gaze.

I mean it. *I don't have time.* But...maybe I should?

CHAPTER ONE

COLE

THE PHANTOM PAIN WOULD STRIKE AT THE STRANGEST times. More often than not, they'd strike when I was feeling good overall. Like today, arriving back in Pineville and the home of my sister. We were all either one had left. Well, that wasn't entirely true. Evie was getting married. A bit fast if you asked me, but no one did. Especially not my hardheaded younger sister.

But she always knew what she wanted. Something completely opposite of our mother. Probably why she'd waited so long to marry. She often told me she'd never settle for just any man. So, although my trip was already planned, I now had another goal: to make sure she hadn't. Settled, that is.

The main reason I'd returned home was to conquer my childhood demons and work on lessening the effects of the PTSD that had been hitching a ride inside me for the past two years. I'd left the Army at thirty-six, two years short of the twenty-year hitch I'd been planning. But you know what they say about plans and life getting in the way. So here I am back in the town I had a love-hate relationship with.

Knocking on her front door, I quickly banished the path my thoughts had turned and scanned the neighborhood. It was a couple steps up from the area we'd grown up in. It had sidewalks. All the yards were well maintained and not a rusted-out project car in sight. It was a family friendly enclave filled with late-model cars and well-maintained jungle gyms made of wood instead of outdated metal.

"Cole!" Evie launched herself at me. She wrapped her arms around my neck, hugging me close. I took a step back to regain my balance, and that's when my left thigh protested. Shifting my weight to my right leg helped ease the pressure on my left leg that had been mangled beyond saving below the knee. The Army docs had no choice but to amputate. I woke in recovery to a new reality and without three of my men; friends, brothers who I would have gladly given my life.

Instead, I'm left with nightmares, months of rehab and two years of therapy. I spent most of my days trying to make sense out of the senseless and find a new purpose.

"Come in. I can't believe you're finally here. Sam's still in court, but he should be able to join us for a late dinner, possibly dessert. He's taken on an extra case so he can manage a week off after we get married for a honeymoon."

Evie let me go, then looked behind me. "I can't believe you still have that old Ford. And you brought your motorcycle...I thought you were going to sell it?"

My sister was the last one who'd suggest I shouldn't ride my bike because of my prosthetic. She knew how much riding meant to me. But she was never a fan of them. When our old man was around, and sober, he'd take me out on rides. But Evie would never go. Probably because she was too young, and the SOB would rev his engine, making her cry.

"I changed my mind. But I won't be riding it anytime soon. It needs some work." My gaze returned to my sister just as a look of relief crossed her face. Chuckling, I swung an arm around her shoulders. "Don't worry so much. You've seen me ride."

"Yeah, that's the problem. I know you. You ride that thing as if it was your last day." His sister gave him a stern look that quickly turned into a huge smile.

He liked seeing her happy. It had been a long time coming.

"I recognize that look, Cole. We're a long way from our childhood, both in years and neighborhoods." She gave me another squeeze, holding me tighter than before. "We got this, big brother. I'm here anytime you need me...well, maybe not during my honeymoon." Her muffled words settled me in a way I hadn't felt since long before I'd left Pineville the first time. Back to when we were young enough to still believe in fairy tales and our small family had been happy.

I'd waited a long time to come back, to put my wellbeing ahead of my service to my country. I may have been forced to leave the Army, but I was determined to find a way to make everything I'd gone through, what my men had sacrificed, mean something.

"C'mon. Stop brooding. I made your favorite." Following Evie inside her house which would now be mine for the foreseeable future, I breathed in the scent of chicken and dumplings, my stomach growled effectively doing its job of making me forget my troubles if only for as long as it took me to eat my sister's home-cooked meal.

She had no idea how much I was looking forward to her fussing over me, cooking my favorite meals from childhood and enjoying some long overdue peace and quiet. A simple plan I could get behind.

CHAPTER TWO

SCARLETT

My shift at O'Malley's Pub was almost over, and I was looking forward to a rare early evening with Matty. "Hey, Scarlett. Mav just called me with the heads up he and a group are on their way over. Could you stick around for another couple hours?"

Darn it, scratch that thought. I could use the extra money and when one of the owners dropped in, the likelihood of larger tips was all but guaranteed. Unfortunately, it also sometimes meant a rowdier crowd. We often had a rush after an Idaho Outlaws home game, especially when word got out that an owner, who also played for the Outlaws, showed up. With the season long over, I sent up a quick prayer that tonight's arrival of Maverick Jansen, the star pitcher of the Outlaws, plus a couple of other players, would go smoothly.

Pulling out my cell from my apron, I called Grams to let her know. She'd probably remind me again about my all-work and no-play life, but I knew she'd be there for Matty no matter.

At thirty-two, I was getting closer to finally getting my MBA after a six-year break, and hopefully soon I'd be able to pay her back for all the hours of free childcare she'd provided. I'm not sure what I would have done without my grams.

After my divorce, she encouraged me to go back to college and finish the degree that I'd given up on when I found myself pregnant shortly after a whirlwind romance and marriage. Me and Johnny had only lasted two years before we called it quits. He'd moved away and given up his parental rights. Not having a father hadn't been an issue until recently when he'd discovered that his new friend had a daddy and he wanted to know when his would be coming back home.

I knew he was better off without a father who didn't want to be in his life. A lie I did my best to convince myself it was true. Matty didn't need to know about his real father, at least not until he was old enough to understand. Not that having your father give up his rights would be easy to understand.

We only needed one broken heart in our family, and I'd gladly live with one to protect my son from feeling as if he was somehow not good enough for his father's love.

Reading Gram's response, I sent off a quick heart emoji, tucked the cell back in my pocket, and greeted a large group of fans.

Stepping up to the bar an hour later, I gave the bartender, Slade, an order. "Hey, another round of the house draft for table twenty."

Slade's gaze flicked toward the loud bunch in the far

corner, then back to me. "They keeping their hands to themselves?"

Sighing, I rolled my eyes. Slade was overprotective, handsome and single, but he'd proclaimed himself my honorary older brother and I was fine with the arrangement. We were friends first and foremost; never crossing that co-worker line to more.

My girlfriends always teased me about him, not believing me that we'd never hooked up. He knew that I was determined to give Matty a better life and myself a career. Not that I felt working at the pub was beneath me because the tips were amazing. This job was a bridge to helping me finish my degree, as it allowed me the flexible work hours I needed. And when I wasn't working at the pub, attending my classes or studying, I would pick up and deliver groceries and meal orders on the weekends.

I knew I was burning the candle at both ends. Sure, I'd sacrificed my social life, but our future was worth it. Matty was my whole world. Had been since the moment he took his first breath. But once I no longer had financial help after Johnny left, I accepted my grandmother's offer to live with her. She needed a roommate so she could keep her house and I had someone to watch Matty for me while I worked. After I'd saved enough money and received a couple small scholarships, I was finally able to go back to school. And now I could see the light at the end of the tunnel. I'd have my degree in less than a year.

"Yes, *Dad*. I think they got the hint when you went over there earlier and gave them the stink eye." I stretched my back to work out the knots. I'd chosen fashion over comfort today with my new boots. I lifted the tray full of drafts and dreamt about having a long soak in the tub tonight after I got home.

Thanks to Slade's intervention, I didn't have to deal with unwanted and obnoxious pickup lines from the group of overzealous fans. They even left me a very generous tip.

As I finished my shift and looked around the nearly empty pub, I noticed a couple so wrapped up in each other they hadn't noticed when I'd dropped off their bill. It was times like this I wished I hadn't shut myself off to dating. A part of me did miss having someone special in my life. Someone who'd look at me the way her customer was looking at his girlfriend.

Not to mention sex. I missed that too. The last time I had it, almost three years ago now, had been so disappointing that I gave up on dating altogether. Whoever said bad sex was better than no sex hadn't been with the last guy I was with. Besides, I was so busy with school, work and my son that finding the right guy seemed too daunting.

Investing in a good vibrator had been a no brainer and would continue to be put to good use for the foreseeable future. It wasn't like I expected my dream man to suddenly show up and sweep me off my feet anytime soon.

CHAPTER THREE

COLE

"Hey MITHTER!"

I was up early. Evie had already left for work, and I was out back enjoying my first cup of coffee of the day. But it wasn't so early that I felt sleep deprived or should be hearing voices. In fact, it'd been a few months since I'd had a dream where one of my men lay dying, calling my name, their voice laced in agony.

Cautiously, I opened one eye and scanned the backyard. No signs of life, no hallucinations—just a crisp fall morning in northern Idaho. I relaxed and took another sip of my Mexican coffee. I'd picked up the taste for the cinnamon laced brew from Beckett, a fellow ranger whose mother made the best enchiladas I'd ever had. He is still serving and my last tether to my old unit.

The coffee was strong and hot just the way I liked it, and it soon began to weave its magic, clearing the fog of a restless night. Leaning back, I soaked in the peace, the silence of the neighborhood. The faraway voice forgotten.

This area was the polar opposite of my last deployment in Afghanistan. Hell, it was just as different as where I'd been living the last two years in a condo in Virginia, too close to the noisy downtown district but convenient to my rehab needs.

"*Mithter*. Whatcha' doin' in Ms. Evie's yard?" A slight lisp accompanied the question. Both eyes popped open this time. I took my time looking across the grass covered yard dotted with a few trees. I didn't have any kids in my life, so dreaming about a child wasn't something I'd ever done and this disembodied voice knew my sister's name. This had to be real and close by. Maybe coming from the next yard?

"You shouldn't be there, *mithter*. I'm telling." This time the voice was louder. Its tone held an unnatural authority for one so young.

I chuckled at the warning. A young member of the neighborhood watch on patrol. Standing, I scanned the fence line on both sides of the yard, before resting on the largest tree. An oak situated in the corner, its branches hanging over the fence and into the eastern neighbor's yard. About eight feet up, on a thick branch, was a child in a blue windbreaker, a mop of auburn hair atop their head holding a toy periscope.

Holding up both hands, I addressed my potential captor. "No need to turn me in. I'm Ms. Evie's brother. She said it was okay if I sat out here."

Loud whispering floated down to me, but I couldn't quite make out the words. What was a kid that young doing up so high? And where were the parents?

The branch quivered, dried leaves fell to the ground as

my young overseer shimmied down the tree, and not on their side of the fence but Evie's.

"You, ah, able to get down, okay?" I raised my voice so if the missing parents happened to be in earshot, they'd be alerted to their offspring's whereabouts.

A pair of sneakers that'd seen better days dangled below the lowest branch. "Uh, *mithter*, I think I'm 'tuck on something."

Of course he was.

This time, I recognized the voice as that of a little boy's and it held a note of panic. Looking down at my foot, I remembered I hadn't bothered with a shoe since I thought I'd only be on the patio, plus I hadn't planned on running this morning. The plan had been to relax. So much for that.

Shrugging, I'd walked over worse landscape in my life. I could handle the frost-covered lawn and scattered leaves. On my way over, I sent up a quick prayer that the kid's mom or dad would suddenly appear and take care of their little adventurer.

Stopping under the tree, I assessed the situation. "Hold on. Let me get a better look and—" Before I could finish my instructions, I had an armful of squirming and excited child.

"That was awesome. I broke free all by myself and you caught me! You must be *thuper* strong and whoa what happened to your leg?"

Dangling sideways in my arms, the boy was staring down at my left leg. He wiggled out of my arms, landing on his feet. Was this kid part cat?

"Are you a pirate or *thomething*?" He was squatting, hands on his knees, his nose scrunched up as he inspected my fancy hardware.

A pirate? Yeah, I guess without the shoe attachment, my

prosthetic looked more like a peg leg, ala Long John Silver, but the kid was too young to get the reference.

"Nope. Definitely not a pirate. Just a guy who lost part of his leg in the..." Dang it. Should I say war? Would this kid even know there had been a war just a couple of years ago? Dammit. I wasn't going to be the one to tell him.

"Uh, I was in an accident and the doctors fixed me up the best they could, but I needed a new leg, well, half a leg."

The boy bounced up and circled me, then squatted back down, taking a closer look. "Can I touch it?"

Before I could move or answer, he poked at the prosthetic. His little head tilted, and a hunk of red hair fell in his eyes. Not satisfied with his first attempt, he did it a second time. "Ow! It's like *thuper* hard. Doesn't it hurt to '*tick* it in your leg?"

"Matthew Oliver Wright!"

The unmistakable call of a worried-slash-frustrated mother rang out.

Matthew's little shoulders slumped. Then he grinned at me. "Busted. That's my mom. Guess I gotta go." Sprinting toward the gate on Evie's side of the fence, he paused. "Can I come back later?" His face filled with hope. "I got more questions."

I should probably say no but something about this kid and his curiosity reminded me of myself…fearless and clueless about the dark side of humanity…something I knew a lot about thanks to a father who'd turned into a mean drunk when I needed him most.

"Yeah, sure. I'll be staying here for a while. But next time, ask your mom for permission first, okay?"

I swear the kid jumped two feet in the air.

"Woot! Thanks, *mithter*." Matthew stepped onto a big rock next to the house, unlatched the gate, and zipped away.

Before I could even think of walking back to the patio and my now cold coffee, a woman appeared at the gate. No, not just a woman, a vision of fresh-from-bed sexy softness wrapped in a pink terry-cloth robe. She had dark auburn curls rioting around her head. Deep blue eyes, pink cheeks and the most kissable mouth I'd ever seen. This beautiful woman crossed her arms and stared me down.

I felt as if the wind had just been knocked out of me. My cock twitched, and my brain disengaged.

Ignoring the obvious warning signs of a protective mama bear, I had to meet this woman. I took a step forward and prayed there was no papa bear.

CHAPTER FOUR

SCARLETT

I took in the giant standing in nothing but a t-shirt and cutoff sweatpants in my neighbor's backyard. Something unexpected slammed into me as I continued to look my fill. Something long dormant had sprung back to life. It began as a tingle at the back of neck, then my fingers began to itch. When my nipples perked up and my lower belly did a funny flip and tiny zaps of awareness flamed, I knew I was in trouble.

An unexpected thought rang out in my head: *Oh, yeah, I'd climb him.*

Where had *that* come from? Reality slammed into me. This man, no matter how hot, was a stranger in my neighbor's backyard. I shook my head to clear it and did my best at sounding intimidating. "What are you doing back here? Where's Evie?"

My head spun from being instantly turned on. I did my best to convey concern at his presence. I was pretty sure I could get away from him if he made a sudden move toward me. All I'd have to do is slam the gate and hightail it back to my house and call for help.

I cursed myself for not keeping my phone on me as I searched for Matty. Not smart. Even in this typically safe and quiet neighborhood.

The sandy-haired giant held up his hands. His face split into a smile, making him more handsome, if that was even possible. Did something happen between Evie and Sam? Was this guy some type of one-night stand revenge? I scanned the patio. No sign of Evie. She was usually at work by this time in the morning, but it didn't hurt to be suspicious.

It wasn't really any of my business, but I liked my neighbor and had been happy for her when she told me about Sam. The last time we talked, they were going to get married, and soon.

"So, where's Evie? Her fiancé, Sam, is going to be here any minute to pick her up. If you don't want anything to happen to you when he gets here, I suggest you start talking." My knees shook as I spoke, and not all of that was from fear. I tried to think if I had anything on me, I could use as a weapon. Checking my pockets, I felt a scrunchy. Darn it. So, all I had on my side was the fib that Sam would be here soon.

"Evie's fine. She's at work. And although I haven't met Sam yet, I'm really looking forward to it. He's made my sister a very happy woman and I'm beyond grateful."

I wasn't usually slow on the uptake, but I hadn't had a full cup of coffee yet and I'd only gotten about five hours of sleep, having done some studying after I finished my late shift at the pub last night.

"Run that by me again. Sister? Evie's your sister?"

The blond god with muscles for days nodded. His face was relaxed and friendly and most important of all, he hadn't attempted to move closer to me. Was he just playing me, lulling me into compliance before he jumped? Sighing at how absurd that sounded, I really needed to stop watching all those murder docuseries.

Taking in a deep, calming breath, I let my gaze run over his features, looking for similarities to Evie, before moving down his upper body and lower. I felt myself blush as I focused in on his midsection, noting a bigger than typical bulge between his legs. Hmm, well, that is...impressive.

I hurried along my inspection and let out a silent "Oh" as I took in his left leg and the prosthetic from the knee down.

There wasn't a foot or shoe attached, but then he didn't have a shoe on his right foot either. He obviously hadn't been up long from the scruff on his jaw and the uncombed yet oddly sexy hair. In a short amount of time, I went from on guard for my son and myself to relieved, and very interested.

Squashing the sudden flush of desire, I noticed similarities to Evie, and their eyes were identical in color—a light blue with dark flecks of gray. He was definitely related to Evie. And that meant off-limits. I began to recall her mentioning a brother who lived on the East Coast. She'd mentioned something about his accident in the service, but I'd forgotten what it had been.

"I'm Cole. I got in last night and I'll be staying through the holidays, maybe longer. It seems she and Sam aren't planning on a long engagement."

We stood there in silence, staring at each other. I wasn't sure if he'd asked me something and I'd missed it, but I felt like a schoolgirl not sure how to act around the most popular boy in school and was damn glad for the thickness of my robe because I felt my nipples go hard as he checked me out. I wasn't used to handsome men paying me this level of attention, and it left me speechless.

"So, you're Matthew's mom?"

Cole put an emphasis on "mom" and I wanted to smack myself. Of course, he'd been waiting for me to give him my name. Duh, he wasn't ogling me in my shortie robe, he was just being polite.

Well, no use getting worked up over a guy, especially a friend's brother. And even if it had been ages since someone had made me forget my own name, I had no time for flirtation or whatever it was we were doing.

"Scarlett. Wright. Scarlett and Matthew. Uh, we call him Matty. Wright. That's our last name." *Oh. My. Lord. I'm an idiot.* "Um, so Matty was back here. I hope he wasn't bothering you?"

"At first, I wasn't sure what was happening, but your little tree climber had me going for a moment. I don't have kids, so I'm not used to finding one eight feet up a tree. Your husband probably taught him how to climb, huh?"

Confused at first about the reference to my ex, I almost missed the most important part of his comment. "Wait, did you just say eight feet? As in up that tree? Over there in the corner. That huge tree?" I pointed to the old oak, but I knew which tree he meant. That little daredevil. He finally did it. He was bound and determined to give me my first gray hair.

I didn't wait for Cole to answer as fear gripped me. "How did he get down?"

The gorgeous man rubbed the back of his neck before he answered. "He, uh, he did his best to get down, then he sort of...well, I was right there, and he got stuck on a branch and suddenly he wasn't anymore. I caught him, though. So, no need to worry."

I spun on my heel and raced back home, not carrying that I'd just left the distractingly sexy man—who was off limits and way out of my league—grinning at me as if he went around catching falling children every day. And who knows, maybe he did. He'd been in the service not that long ago.

But right now, I had a five-year-old to ground and get to kindergarten in the next twenty minutes. And wasn't it just my bad luck that the first guy I had an instant, intense attraction to was someone who was only here for the holidays and the brother of my next-door neighbor—definitely unobtainable.

CHAPTER FIVE

COLE

I jerked awake. Cold sweat covered my body, and my heartbeat was thundering. The nightmare was unexpected, but not a real surprise. Seeing the kid dangling from the large oak yesterday, then falling into my arms, had surely triggered it.

Ripping the sheets off me, I sat on the edge of my bed, staring at the hardware that'd become a daily reminder of the worst day of my life and yet a lifeline I'd be forever grateful. Blocking out the dregs of my dream, the chaos, the screams and smells from two years ago, I began the breathing exercises my therapist back home had taught me. I'd refused to be medicated. I didn't want numbness. I wanted to remember the sacrifice my men had made. The brothers in arms who would never breathe, laugh, or know the sweet touch of a woman again—I needed to make my survival mean something in their honor.

At the thought of a woman's touch, Scarlett's image and

her curves replaced the nightmarish visions reminding me of the other reason I tossed and turned most of the night. She was just my type, curvy and full of just the right amount of sass. But there was one tiny thing. I didn't get clear confirmation that she was single. I noticed she wasn't wearing a wedding ring, but that wasn't a given there wasn't a man in her life.

Typically, I steered away from women with kids or if they had them, I always made it clear I wasn't looking to become a stand in daddy. After what I went through with my old man, I'd decided at a very young age that marriage and kids would not be in my future. Besides, I'd yet to find a woman who was worth tempting fate and genetics, much to Evie's frustration. Hopefully, she wouldn't use her upcoming marriage to Sam as ammunition to pester me about my choice to remain single.

I attached my running blade. I had some pavement to pound. And some thinking to do.

All forms of exercise had been my go-to when I needed stress relief. Another tool I used to battle the PTSD that was always on a low simmer and running was my favorite.

In the kitchen I started the coffeemaker, then opened the fridge. I stood there staring for almost a minute before I realized I didn't know what the *eff* I was looking for. Scarlett's curves kept racing through my head. Never had I been so wrapped up in a woman this quick. All I could think about was how I could see her again and find out if she was single.

Pounding erupted from the front door. Now what?

"Hey, *mithter*. Mom's having trouble with our car. Can you help?" Matty's expression was so full of hope, how could I turn him down?

"Sure, kid. Lead the way."

Calling him "kid" even though I now knew his name was deliberate. In a matter of minutes yesterday, Matty had tunneled his way under the permanent line in the sand I had drawn forever ago. I needed to remember why I'd done it, no matter what.

Following him across the lawn, I zeroed in on Scarlett's car. She didn't look up at our approach, most likely unaware that Matty had headed to my sister's house looking for me.

Bending at the waist, I knocked on the driver's side window. Startled, she jumped, her hand covered her face. She took her time in facing me.

Although her expression was full of frustration, her beauty still shined. I watched intently as a pretty pink flush appeared on her cheeks.

The window of her well used SUV rolled down. "Hi. Um, what's up?"

I nodded toward Matty, who was jumping up and down beside me. "A little birdy told me you were having car trouble."

Indecision replaced her frustration. I couldn't blame her reaction. She'd met me less than a day ago and now here I was offering my help, for her and her son, again. Other than knowing I was Evie's brother; she didn't know anything about me other than what she could see. That thought had me immediately wondering what she thought of me and my missing lower leg.

I'd come across many women in the last two years who wouldn't give me the time of day when they saw my prosthetic limb. Then again, I'd pretty much been a monk since the day that took my men along with a chunk of my flesh and bone.

It would be interesting to see if she would now do the same. Before, she had no choice in speaking with me. I'd already helped her son. But now? Would she see me as a capable man who could do the same things other men could? Or would she treat me as damaged, a disabled vet incapable of even the basic of tasks?

I pulled back from her window, frowning at the direction my thoughts had taken, I shook off the momentary self-pity and forced a smile. "Or maybe you already figured out a solution. Either way, just wanted to make sure you were okay."

Scarlett ran a hand through her long, loose hair that appeared freshly washed, and sighed. "Yeah, that would be a big no. I know nothing about cars. I've never had trouble with this one. But it's going on twenty years old, so I guess it could be anything?"

Her uncertainty grabbed me. I knew I wasn't going to just let her flounder out here. If I could help, I would. But like her, I knew little about cars, other than I knew better than to try and fix anything. I let the experts do what they were trained to do.

But I did have a fix to the immediate problem.

"Hey, kid. Grab your stuff and head over to my truck. I'm going to drive you and your mom wherever you need to go."

"Oh, but—" Scarlett sputtered.

"Woo-hoo!" Matty let out the whoop, drowning out his mother's protest. I watched, grinning at his antics as he raced to the passenger side of the car, grabbed his backpack, and was halfway to my old Ford before his mom could exit the car.

"Matty, slow down. Wait for Mr. Nolan before you get inside."

Scarlett stood next to me, closer than she had been yesterday. Much closer. And my body noticed immediately.

She barely reached my shoulder, and my protective instincts kicked in. She was close enough I could feel her body heat, smell her sweet scent. My fingers itched to trace her soft curves, which were perfect, as if made just for me—to caress and fold into my hardness. I had to get my mind off what I wanted and focus on what she needed and fast, otherwise I might do something stupid like kiss her.

I put my hand behind her and indicated she proceed before me. Not totally unselfish of me. I wanted another look at her backside. The urge to watch her walk away overrode any shred of gallantry I may have possessed. Wanting to watch her hips sway and needed to check out her ass like I needed my next breath.

When I did, I briefly closed my eyes and called myself all kinds of fool.

"Cole, thank you so much for this. I'll call a tow truck on the way to Matty's school. We sold my grandmother's car last year to cover her unexpected medical bills, otherwise I'd have another vehicle to use." She peeked back at me, tucking a piece of her dark red hair behind an ear, and smiled. "It's not too far away so we should be back in no time, and you can get back to..." She waved a hand toward me, and I watched captivated as her gaze traveled from my face to my chest to my exposed arms in the old cutoff t-shirt I'd thrown on to going running in then to my exposed thighs.

Her gaze stopped on my blade and her mouth formed an adorable "O" then her eyes flashed, and she grinned.

"That's some pretty impressive hardware. How many prosthetics do you have?"

Before I could answer, the air filled with Matty's singsong voice. "Mom, *mithter*, we're gonna be late. C'mooooooon!"

I chuckled.

She groaned.

"I'm not sure where he gets that from. Honest. Guess we'd better go."

I waited for her to start moving again so I could look my fill. Dangerous for sure, considering the kid was watching, but this woman ticked off all the boxes for me. I sucked in a breath as I watched her move.

Big mistake.

My dick hardened, and I had no way of hiding my instant reaction to her. I turned away for a moment and forced myself to think about anything but her. I closed my eyes and pictured the first time I got a good look at my mangled leg. Instantly, it did the trick, but I knew I'd probably pay the price later for dredging up that particular memory.

I made it to the truck just in time to see Scarlett helping her son into the passenger seat. And it hit me; I didn't have a car seat or one of those booster seats. As I had the thought, she held up a hand. "I'll be right back."

Don't look. Don't look. I managed somehow to keep my focus on the kid. He was looking up at me, smiling.

"So, what grade are you in?" I started the engine and tapped my hands on the steering wheel.

"Grade? No grade. I'm in *kidgarden*," he said beaming with pride.

Damn if his upturned freckled face and shock of red hair didn't tug at my heartstrings.

Scarlett appeared with his booster seat, getting him situated on the bench seat between us. "Matty, it's pronounced kin-der-gar-ten, honey."

Nodding, Matty said, "I know, but '*kidgarden*' is fun to say."

I barked out a laugh and ruffled his hair. "I agree, Matty. And I hope you have a fun day at '*kidgarden.*'

Backing out of the driveway, a shared look passed between us. I saw a flash of interest flare in Scarlett's blue eyes before she turned her attention back to her son. Score one in my favor. Actually, it was two.

When she'd still been in her car, her hands gripping tight on the steering wheel, I was able to take note that she was wearing a couple of rings, but none on her left ring finger.

After we dropped off Matty at his school, a sexually charged silence filled the truck cab. At least, that's how I was feeling. Not sure what was going through her beautiful head. But there was only one way to find out.

"Is there anywhere you need to go? I may not be able to fix your car, but I'd be happy to drive you." Glancing out of the corner of my eye, I let my gaze roam over her body as she squirmed in her seat.

Was she feeling anything close to what I was, and would she be interested in someone like me?

CHAPTER SIX

SCARLETT

It was eight p.m. I was two hours into my five-hour shift at O'Malley's and I still couldn't stop thinking about this morning. And Cole Nolan. He'd kept me from getting a full night's rest. His gravelly voice and heated glances filled my dreams. And now the hunky brother of our sweet neighbor was keeping me from fully focusing on my job. I'd already messed up two drink orders, and that wasn't like me.

"Hey, Red! Yo...we...need another round...over here." A loud burp rang out from the table full of increasingly obnoxious men.

The shouted demand pulled me back to reality. The pub's clientele was usually pretty civil. Oh, we had our share of unruly drunks, but one thing the owners didn't put up with was rude people. It was rule number one. If any of the staff was being mistreated, the manager, or the lead bartender, would handle any situation, protecting the employees, especially the female staff, from any verbal or physical harm.

And today, this customer had chosen poorly. Because behind the bar was one of the owners. It was the off season and so it was more likely that either Maverick Jansen or Luke Garibaldi would be pulling drafts for a few hours and chatting with the pub's regulars. The United States Baseball League's premier players from the local Idaho Outlaws enjoyed working their business whenever time allowed.

I released a sigh and looked over my shoulder. Luke sent me a nod, then pointed a finger and mouthed, "I got this." I watched as the Outlaw's catcher made his way over to the table filled with biker wannabes were seated.

I walked in the opposite direction and headed to the bar where Taya, our head chef, was speaking to Slade. I settled in next to her. She bumped me on the hip and grinned. "We're so lucky to work here." She nodded her head in the direction Luke had gone.

Taya had been working here for about a year and was one of the reasons for the uptick in business. She'd elevated pub food to a new level and word had spread. Like me, she was also a single mom, but to look at her you'd never know she was in her mid-forties and had kids in college.

"Yeah, and he's not hard on the eyes either." I sent her a wink, then chuckled. It was an old joke and certainly not something I would act on. Luke was married, so was Maverick, but both men were fit and handsome and I was only human. So yeah, it wasn't a hardship to work at O'Malley's.

"Amen to that." Taya took her soft drink from Slade and held it up in a salute. "Here's to you and me finding some equally fine men and may they treat us as well as they treat their wives." I returned her gesture with a mock salute of my own.

Looking over my shoulder, Taya's eyes widen. "Oh, my. I didn't think my prayers would be answered quite so soon."

With Slade's laughter ringing in my ears, I turned to see what she meant and came face-to-face with Cole.

And he was dressed. Wait. that didn't sound right. He was wearing long pants and a shirt with sleeves. If you didn't know about his leg, you couldn't tell he wore a prosthetic. And he made my heart stutter. His hair had been combed with something other than his fingers and he was wearing a dark grey, tight fit V-neck that defined his upper muscles in a way that should be illegal. His jeans were a dark stone wash that hugged his tree trunk thighs. Hard bodied men had never been her type—until now.

"Cole. Hi. What are you doing here?" Wow, that came out harsh.

He didn't respond to my question. Instead, he was staring at Slade who had gone quiet behind me.

"Hi, I'm Taya. A friend of Scarlett's. Welcome to O'Malley's. I recommend the Wagyu beef sliders with a zesty horseradish aioli and the house draft. And I, oh..." She looked between me and Cole, then over to Slade before stepping closer to me and whispering. "You've been holding out on me. That man is staking his claim. Poor Slade."

Poor Slade? Wait, this was getting out of hand. I needed to correct her. Cole and I had nothing going on. But before I could, Taya patted me on the arm and hurried back into the kitchen.

I continued to look between Cole and Slade. What the heck was up? Surely Cole, or Slade for that matter, wasn't jealous.

"Um, yeah. So, Cole, this is Slade Johansson, one of the best bartenders at O'Malley's. Slade, this is Cole Nolan. His sister is my next-door neighbor, and he's in town for Thanksgiving and her upcoming wedding."

Slade lifted his chin. "Nice to meet you. Scarlett, if you want to take a break, I can handle any new customers that come in."

Cole's gaze flicked back to me. He smiled but didn't say anything to correct Slade's assumption that he was here just to see me.

"I, uh...you can take a seat at the bar or if you want a table, I've got a couple two seaters open." The intensity of his gaze had me clenching my thighs together and wringing my hands. How did he do that? Turn me on with just a look. Surely, I was reading him wrong. Men like him never went for women like me.

I'd convinced myself earlier he was just being nice by offering me a ride home after my shift tonight. I never thought he'd show up. I still had ninety minutes before the end of my shift.

"A table would be great. I didn't come in expecting you to wait on me, though. I'm on my own for dinner. Evie's at Sam's place and I didn't feel like cooking."

Right. I knew there had to be a reason. He wasn't here to see me. He was just hungry. Sure, he could have eaten anywhere in Pineville, but this made sense, given his offer to drive me home later.

I handed him a menu after he sat down. "Take your time. You heard Taya's suggestion. If you're a slider fan, they are the best. And she makes the aioli fresh daily. It's one of our best seller's."

He smiled. I swear his eyes twinkled at me and I melted. Get a grip Scarlett. He's just here for the food. But a girl could dream, right? His blue eyes, darker than mine, had speckles of grey and white and I could get lost in them if I looked long enough.

"Scarlett?"

The sound of my name on his lips warmed me all over. I shivered at the thought of how deep his voice would sound if we were wrapped up in each other, straining to get closer and...

"Sweetie, you keep staring at me like that and I'm going to pull you into my lap and fulfill whatever it is that you're thinking about. No sane man in his right mind would turn down the invitation written all over your face." He adjusted himself, proving he was as affected as I was. "And Scarlett, all you have to do is say the word. Right here, right now."

Oh. My. Lord. Did Cole just say he wanted me? Like he wanted to do to me what I so desperately wanted him to do to me since the moment we dropped my son off at school this morning.

This was too crazy. I just met this man and he had me so tied up in knots and my sexual fantasies I was contemplating taking him up on his offer.

"Don't think too hard. I'm only joking. Mostly. I'm not sure what is happening between us, Scarlett, and I'm not asking you for a commitment. But it's been a long time, if ever, that a woman has me constantly hard the way you do. Hell, I even dreamed about you last night and what I wanted to do with you, so if you're not interested, let me know and I'll back off."

I watched as he again shifted in his seat, and I just had to know. What were we doing in his dreams?

It wasn't like I was some inexperienced girl. I was a woman with needs and the more time I spent around him; I sensed he'd be able to fulfill them. I stepped closer to the table, to him, and looked down at his lap.

Cole had an unmistakable bulge straining behind his zipper. As my gaze locked on it, I heard a low growl emit from his chest. Our eyes clashed, and in that moment, there was no turning back.

Except for one thing. I didn't have time for him or whatever this was between us. This instant connection. I wasn't looking for anything permanent either. Not right now. Maybe once I had my degree, a good-paying job and a place of my own, with Matty. But a relationship wasn't on my radar.

All my free time needed to be spent studying for semester finals. And on top of that, now I needed to ask for extra shifts so I could pay the repair bill, which would leave little to no time to even think about hooking up with my neighbor's hot brother.

And yet, how could I deny what was clearly happening between us? The unexpected sexual tension had me thinking that I deserved to live on the edge, take something for myself and Cole Nolan was what I wanted.

But first I had one question. Okay, two. Maybe three.

CHAPTER SEVEN

SCARLETT

"Before I decide. Why are you here? I mean in Pineville. Are you planning on living next door or...?" I couldn't quite finish the sentence because then he might think I was looking for more than he was offering. I wasn't. I simply didn't want to voice it in a crowded pub.

Cole's eyebrows went up at my rapid-fire questions. "I'm not sure how long I'll be at Evie's, but I don't plan on staying long. I'm in town for a lot of reasons. Thanksgiving for one and now it seems I'll be giving her away." He paused, rubbed a hand over his jaw, and sighed. "And I have some things to work out...but I'd like nothing more than to explore this intense connection between us. But I'm not going to make any promises I can't keep. Hell, I'm still dealing with...stuff from my last deployment. I don't think either one of us is looking for long term anyway, right?"

His question shouldn't have caused my stomach to drop,

but it did. His words echoed my thoughts. I didn't need pretty words or fake promises.

I shook my head. "No. My life is busy and now with no car, it's going to get busier. So, whatever this is, this thing between us—"

"I get it. So, we take it a day at a time, when you have time, okay?"

My head bobbed again. "Sure. I have some time tonight after my shift, but my place is out of the question. I don't bring men home." *Shit. Did I just say that?*

"Ever?" he asked.

"Never. I have two roommates. Makes it a bit difficult to scratch an itch, you know?"

Cole's face lit up. "Well, it seems I'm going to have the house to myself. Evie told me she's pretty much moved into Sam's condo and they're planning on buying a place together after they get married."

The unspoken invitation hung in the air. I wasn't going to pretend I didn't know what he meant. So the only thing to do was decide if I would take him up on his offer?

I didn't allow any time to talk myself out of it. I matched his smile and took back the menu. "I'll put in your order with the kitchen and get you the house draft." Walking away from him, my body heated, and my heart skipped at the thought of being alone with Cole.

I hustled between tables, delivering food and drinks, but the whole time my mind was on him. And after almost sixty long minutes of trading heat filled glances, Cole led me out to his truck parked in the furthest slot in the back parking lot of the pub.

We both reached for the passenger door handle at the same time, and I swear an arc of electricity zapped from his hand to mine. The feeling went straight to my breasts. My nipples tingling, then my clit pulsed, demanding attention.

He swore.

I sucked in a noisy breath.

And in a flash, I was pinned between hard steel.

The door panel was at my back, Cole to my front and his erection pressed against my lower belly. All good sense was replaced by a driving need to have him inside of me. I didn't have a chance to voice my wants. His lips captured mine and oh, *yes, please*. I've never been kissed so desperately, hungrily before. His tongue mastered mine, and I moaned. Ecstasy ran unchecked through me.

I clung to his waist, his hands tunneled through my hair, tugging me closer and our lower bodies fused despite the barrier of clothing.

One kiss and I was addicted to him.

His taste. His touch. His hot body as it cradled and dominated me. My hips began to rock against his thigh, my panties now drenched. I ached for him. I no longer cared we were outside my work where anyone could see us. I needed this, him. It'd been so long since I'd allowed myself to let go with a man that my sex starved body was ramped so high, the desperation to come took over every thought I had.

I could have cried when he pulled back, breaking our kiss. Our heavy breathing filled the air. Cole pressed his forehead on mine, letting out a groan I felt all the way to my toes.

"I didn't mean for that to happen, Scarlett. Damn. Get in the truck."

The phrase dazed and confused suddenly had a new meaning. I watched him as he lifted me onto the bench seat, buckled me in and shut the door in my face without saying a word. He climbed into the driver's seat, then squealed out of the parking lot. Stunned at the need he created within me and his reaction, I stared straight ahead as he attempted a new land speed record back to our neighborhood.

Less than five minutes later, he pulled into his driveway, shut off the engine, and ran a hand down his face. "I'm on edge here, Scarlett. If you want to finish what we just started, follow me inside. If not, I suggest you get out now and lock your door behind you because I'm harder than I've ever been. Burying myself into you is all I can focus on."

His declaration sounded like a dare. Oh, I was all in. I didn't answer him. I stumbled out of the truck and raced to the front door. The sound of his slamming door followed me. He caught up to me as I reached the porch. He wrapped an arm around my waist, lifted me slightly, then fumbled the key in the lock.

Once inside, he didn't stop. Not to lock the door, not to make sure Evie wasn't home. He marched us to the back bedroom, crossed the threshold, kicked the door shut and set me down at the foot of the bed.

"Strip." Cole's gravelly voice commanded.

I did. And I watched as he did the same. Then he sat down on the edge of the bed, his magnificent chest on full display. My eyes greedily took him in as he worked his jeans down his legs, exposing his beefy thighs, and the cloth hugging his left limb. He caught my gaze before letting his gaze drift down my electrified body. There I was, naked as the day I was born, not a shred of embarrassment to let him see all my imperfections. In the past, with the few lovers I've had, just the thought of being so vulnerable would normally overwhelm me. Heck, I'd never let even Matty's dad see me completely nude.

Cole let out a low growl. My nipples perked up, and a fresh pool of warmth settled between my thighs.

"Fuck, woman. You're a goddess."

I almost wept at his declaration.

"Okay, I've never done this in front of anyone before. If you don't want to watch, I'll understand." He tore his gaze from me and began removing his prosthetic.

As if I could look away. I dropped to my knees and put a hand on his forearm. When the limb was totally bare, I swept my fingers lightly over the damaged skin, then bent forward and placed a kiss on the puckered skin. He jumped at the contact and let loose another throaty growl.

"C'mon here, baby." He lifted me up, and I straddled his lap. His cock pressing at my entrance—and there was no more talking. Only feeling. Accepting each other. A sudden need to show this man he was so much more than his injury overtook me. What had happened to him was terrible, but it didn't define him. Any more than my curvy body defined me.

To me, he was the sexiest man I could have ever dreamed of.

His lips latched onto a hard nipple and one of his hot hands circled the other breast, caressing it and pinching its tip. The action ignited a slow roll in my belly. My hips rotated, and I pressed down onto his erection, seeking sweet bliss.

He laid back, still suckling me. I followed, bracing my hands on either side of his head. The movement created a sharp zing on my clit and all I could think about was impaling myself on his impressive cock. As I thought about it, Cole moved both hands to my waist and pulled me up to his chest.

"I need to taste you. Make you come on my face." His demand made me wetter.

But I hesitated as shyness hit me. I stopped moving. "I've never—"

"Shh, it's okay. I've got you. Just let yourself go and hold on tight to the headboard." He nudged me toward his lips. His hot breath tickled me, stoking the flame between us, and I moaned. God, yes. I wanted this.

Spreading my thighs wide, I gripped the headboard and lowered myself down.

He cradled my ass, pulling me closer, then dived between my folds. His teeth scraped my swollen bud and I let out a groan. "Oh.... Yes...yes."

My orgasm built. Forgotten was any hint of insecurity.

As Cole stroked me, his murmured words of encouragement stoked my pleasure, and I began to move faster against his wicked tongue. Soon a sharp tingle began deep within me, and I rode it, pressing down, chasing it until I lost my breath and the orgasm slammed into me. Then I was crying out Cole's name over and over. My throat raw, I collapsed onto his chest, his large, warm hands stroking my back as bursts of delicious aftershocks rocked me.

"I hadn't planned on this. I don't have any protection. But I haven't been with anyone since before my accident."

Cole's words broke through the fog of the most intense orgasm I'd ever had. And his erection pulsed beneath me, reminding me how much I wanted him to fill me and give him the same pleasure I'd just received.

"Me either. I mean, I'm clean. I haven't been with anyone longer than that." Discussing such intimate details no longer seemed embarrassing. All I wanted was Cole inside of me and if that meant he would need to pull out, I was very much on board.

"Are you ready for me? I mean, I can wait if you need me to."

I slid over his cock and chuckled. "Oh, I'm ready."

He flipped me over, grabbed himself and guided his cock into me. Bracing himself on one knee, he filled me to the hilt. I wrapped my legs around him, lifted my hips. Pounding into me, his strokes sparked the beginning of another orgasm. We rocked into each other. He kissed me senseless once again and the thought of never wanting this feeling to end turned over and over in my mind.

When Cole pinched my clit, I exploded. My inner walls squeezed him tight. But he was unrelenting and kept stroking me with his thumb until another orgasm overtook me. My entire body vibrated, and then he shouted my name. I almost wept when he pulled out, but his whispered words in my ear assured me he was just as satisfied as I was.

I fell asleep wrapped tight in his arms, our legs entwined. My first thought was when could we do that again? I must have spoken it out loud because I felt his chest rumble from a very sexy laugh, then his arms squeezed me closer.

This felt so right, and I was so in trouble.

CHAPTER EIGHT

SCARLETT

Stretching, I rolled to my side and smiled. Last night had been...words still failed me hours later, but wow was a good start. I could use another couple of hours of sleep, but caffeine and a hot shower would have to do.

Today was Thanksgiving, and I was making dinner this year after I put my foot down with Grams that I was happy to take over the cooking duties. On the upside, I didn't have to work today, and was even giving myself a break from studying. I'd left Cole softly snoring last night and snuck back into my house shortly after midnight. I'd never had to be quiet so late before.

Coffee was the first item on my to-do list, then a quick shower before I prepped our meal.

"So, I hear Evie's brother is in town?" Grams' question had me jumping a foot in the air and nearly out of my skin. She stood in the doorway, an innocent look on her face.

"You're up early. I told you I'd take care of everything this year." I poured us both a cup of coffee and handed her one so she could doctor it up the way she liked it.

Grams shuffled over to the fridge, then to the kitchen table, and sat. We both sipped in silence, allowing the magic beans to do their work.

I knew she was waiting for me to say something about Cole, but I wasn't quite ready to share considering how short a time it took me from lusting after the man to ending up in his bed. I felt myself flushing at the memory of the two of us together.

Grams let out a funny snort and my gaze snapped to her face. She wore a crooked and knowing grin. "It may have been a long while since a man put a look on my face like the one you're wearing, but I'm not so old I don't know the signs. Good for you. You deserve to have someone that can make you blush."

To say that I was shocked didn't cut it. Grams wasn't one for discussing intimate things. The furthest she went was stating I needed to begin dating again. I decided to turn the conversation in a different direction. I was not going to discuss my sex life with my grandmother.

"So, how'd you know about her brother?" I began gathering items for the stuffing since it seemed a shower would have to wait.

"Matty. He was fairly vibrating the other day with excitement, describing how this huge man next door with a metal leg caught him before he fell on his head out of Evie's oak tree. And then he tells me Mr. Cole drove him to school yesterday."

I winced when she put emphasis on the word "fell." At the time, I hadn't seen a reason to tell her about the incident since Matty hadn't been injured. She was even more protective of my son than I was, but at eighty-three, I didn't want her worrying more about him than she already did.

I pasted a smile on my face and turned. "Sorry I didn't tell you. It's been a busy couple days with the car crapping out and it slipped my mind."

"Mm, hmm. Well, I got a good look at him yesterday when he was out jogging. He was wearing this curved metal attachment on his leg. Can you imagine such a thing? But he was running just like any other fool person who decided to waste their heartbeats that way. But he's got some nice muscles, yes, he does. He's a looker, Scarlett. And he's single too." Grams looked out the window over the sink into our backyard, taking another sip of her coffee.

I could feel her wheels turning under her pink-tinted grey curls. She was waiting for me to spill my guts. But how did you let your grandmother know you already knocked boots with the hot guy next door and not have her singing the wedding march? I wasn't sure how she would feel about hooking up with a guy just for sex. Not expecting anything more than some fun and orgasms. And oh, there'd been orgasms. More than I'd ever had in one night.

But I knew what I'd signed up for. Nothing serious. Neither one of us were looking for happily ever after, but as long as he was next door, I wouldn't say no to a few more nights with him.

"Well, I know you don't want or need me in your personal life. But I'd like to see you with a nice man. Someone who's good to you and Matty. I want to go to my maker knowing you two are taken care of, sweetie."

My heart melted. I knew she wanted what was best for me and Matty. She'd been there for me after my dad left my mom, then again when mom had passed from breast cancer when I was twenty. That was the first time I had to put college on hold. The second was when I met my ex after finally going back to school, but our whirlwind romance and elopement had resulted in an unplanned pregnancy and once again I had to leave my dream of earning an MBA.

Grandma was old school and had been pushing me to date, find someone to support me so I could stay home with Matty. She didn't understand my drive to earn a degree, so I could take care of the two of us on my own.

"I know Grams. I'm so close to my degree, though. Just one more semester and I'll be able to go after my dream job, stop waiting tables and delivering groceries. I'm only thirty-two and besides, there's no age limit on falling in love, or finding someone to spend the rest of my life with."

I needed to get her off this subject and now. "How about I make you some scrambled eggs, then I'm banning you from the kitchen. I need you to keep Matty entertained." Walking over to her, I placed a kiss on top of her head and hugged her.

"I love you, Grams."

"I love you too, Scarlett. Can't blame an old woman for trying."

No, I couldn't.

I made a panful of scrambled eggs for both her and Matty. He'd be up soon and hungry. I managed to shoo them both out of the kitchen after they ate, stuffed the bird and got it into the oven.

Later, as I stood under a spray of hot water, I allowed my mind to wander back to Cole and last night. I had no way of contacting him unless I wanted to knock on his front door. I hadn't thought about giving him my cell number or asking for his. I knew he'd be with his sister and her fiancé today for Thanksgiving, but a small part of me wanted to ask him over.

It was too dangerous to be thinking of him at all beyond what we shared. It was just sex. That's all it could be.

CHAPTER NINE

COLE

Time was a funny thing. For months after the explosion and losing my men, then learning to walk with the prosthetic, the days, weeks and months dragged. I began to believe anything good, anything lasting couldn't happen fast. And I settled into that mind frame, in part thanks to the help of the many doctors and fellow servicemen and women I went through rehab with. I clung to it, believing all I had to do was give myself enough time to heal.

But now my life had changed in an instant. From the very moment a precocious kid and curvy woman appeared unexpectedly.

I'd been doing plenty of thinking lately. Back to after I first came stateside after my injury. Evie had been there for me in the beginning. She made sure I ate, got to my therapy appointments and didn't fall into a black hole of depression. After she left, I began seeing a therapist who helped me find ways to battle the PTSD from becoming all-consuming.

But I needed to take another step in my recovery. I needed to face the childhood memories that had reemerged. My dad had died four years ago, and shortly after I received the biggest shock of my life. Evie had called to tell me he had a life insurance policy listing us as beneficiaries. It was a large enough amount of money I didn't need to worry about working for at least a decade.

For a while, all the money did was piss me off. Why had he taken care of us in death, but he couldn't have spared a kind word or deed when we'd been kids? Finally, I just became so weary of all the anger, I buried it. Until now.

He wasn't worth the energy I was putting into hating him. Although, I hadn't seen him since my eighteenth birthday, the day before I shipped out for boot camp, part of me regretted leaving Evie behind, but mom had still been alive then and dad didn't treat my sister nearly as bad as he did me.

I'd tried for years to banish him from my mind, but anytime I doubted myself during my career, the demons of doubt sowed by his overblown paranoia whenever he drank overwhelmed me. And since he drank every day to excess, my therapist helped me see that I'd been living with PTSD even before stepping on a battlefield.

So why was I hesitating to follow through on one of the main reasons I'd come home? Because life had suddenly taken a turn for the better. I'd become so wrapped up in Scarlett over the past ten days, I'd set it aside.

Ten days of listening to her sweet sighs and demanding shouts for more when I was balls deep inside her.

Ten days of seeing her as a mother and interacting with Matty had quickly become the highlight of my days.

Ten days of conversations that seemed lighthearted on

the surface but showed me what a good person she was as well as funny, smart and caring.

The fact we didn't just spend time in bed where it was simple to confine our relationship to just sex had me questioning my promise to keep it uncomplicated because each day my need to be with her grew.

After a week and a half of picking her up from the pub where we both knew how the night would end—in my bed—something big within me shifted. I didn't want to name it for fear of breaking the spell. It was as if my life now had purpose, a new purpose beyond my years as an Army ranger, and it scared the shit out of me.

Today we're picking up Matty from '*kidgarten*' and I still didn't know how to handle these new feelings.

"Hey, Mr. Cole. Is it okay if you drop me off at my friend Riley's house? We're going to play catch. Do you know how to catch a baseball? If you do, maybe we could play catch too?" Matty ran out of breath from his rapid-fire questioning. My gaze flicked to Scarlett. She finished settling him into his booster seat then sent me an apologetic smile.

I mouthed, "Don't worry." A sudden urgency overcame me to reassure her that her son was no bother. When I opened my mouth to let him know I'd love to play catch, Matty turned to me, his eyes lit up in anticipation making me momentarily speechless. This kid was something else. I didn't have a lot of experience with children, but he was quickly carving out a Matty-sized space in my heart.

"Annnnd Mom already said I could go. And Riley's mom is going to drive me home." Matty tipped his chin up, steepled his fingers in prayer, then put the final point in his plea with a drawn out "*pleaaaaase?*"

This kid always had me smiling and/or chuckling.

"Well, how could I say no to '*pleaaaaase?*' And we can play catch whenever you want." I mimicked his hand position and exaggeration and then I did something without thinking. I began tickling him in the ribs until he squealed. The sound could have been piercing, but to me it was pure joy to my ears, a tonic for my wounded soul.

And I ate it up since today was the last day I'd be driving Matty anywhere. I was taking Scarlett to pick her car up from the mechanic right after.

As Matty settled down, I caught Scarlett's reaction. Her lips were curled up at the corners in a sweet smile, but her eyes were filled with unshed tears. I found myself wanting to lean over the top of Matty and kiss her tears away. But I knew that was stepping over an imaginary line that would raise too many questions and confuse the still giggling boy.

And it didn't sit well with me. Not one bit. I wanted everyone, especially Matty, to know how I felt about Scarlett. I didn't want to hide what we'd been doing. Falling asleep with her every night, only to wake up alone the next morning had become so damn hard.

I found myself wanting to talk to her after I read something in the paper that sparked my interest or when I discovered a new restaurant and wanted to take her out. But I didn't because we were just having fun.

But at that moment, I realized that was no longer enough for me. I wanted more, so much more, from her. In shock, it hit me harder than a ton of bricks. I'd fallen in love with Scarlett.

"Hey, Mr. Cole, can we leave now?"

I blinked slowly, trying to remember what came next. Oh yeah. I was taking him to his friend's house, then Scarlett to the repair shop.

"Uh, sure. You bet."

Scarlett rattled off the directions as I drove and, before I realized where we were headed, I turned left onto a street I knew all too well.

I slowed to almost a crawl as my childhood home caught my eye. The address we needed was three houses further down, but I couldn't take my eyes off the single-story craftsman that had obviously been updated. The front yard was well taken care of compared to when my family lived there and instead of a banged up old boat on the side of the house there was now a pad of cement and a basketball hoop.

"Cole? You okay? Riley's house is just down the street on the right."

"I see him. I see him, Mom. He's in the driveway." Matty started hopping up and down in his seat and waving.

"I see him, Matty. Now sit still." Scarlett settled Matty down.

"Cole, the house is just up ahead." Her words broke me out of my fog and from the corner of my eye, I noticed concern on her face as I turned my attention back to the road.

I'd planned on visiting the old neighborhood, but not this soon, and certainly not with an audience. My gut was in knots and I felt as if the wind had been knocked out of me.

Now was not the time to freak out, not with Matty and Scarlett watching. I dug deep to control my emotions and pulled up to the friend's house.

Staring straight ahead the entire time Scarlett spoke with the other kid's mother, her words barely registered after she got back into the truck.

"Yeah, sure." I answered absently, not really sure what she'd just asked me.

Scarlett was quiet the entire drive to the repair shop after a few attempts at engaging me in conversation. I didn't have it in me to reassure her everything was fine. Because it wasn't. Emotionally, I was on the edge of a cliff and if I started speaking, I was sure she'd recognize it and want to help.

But there was no helping me right now.

I needed to be alone and figure my shit out. And I knew I needed to talk to my sister first. I had a lot to make up for with her, even if she didn't agree with me. Because I knew from the sessions I had with my therapist, that if I didn't talk this out, it would eat me up and keep me from moving on with my life.

And I wanted to face my past because, quite possibly, my future was biting her lip and taking quick peeks at me. I knew I was being an ass, but I knew if I opened up now about the reason for my sudden mood change, it would come out wrong and I might screw things up worse than I was doing by remaining silent.

It killed me to see the hurt in her eyes. She thanked me for the ride and exited the truck. I had to hand it to her though. She squared her shoulders and refused to look back at me. Good for her. And hell, I wouldn't have faulted her if she wanted to punch me in the face.

The fact that she hadn't gave me hope that I could fix this. But first I had to get my head right.

CHAPTER TEN

COLE

I'd hurt Scarlett's feelings, but I'd make it up to her. I'd spend the rest of my life making it up to her. After I'd dropped her off, I texted Evie and asked her to dinner. Just the two of us. That was yesterday. My head still pounded from the intense conversation with my sister. I began the dinner apologizing to her for leaving her alone with our drunk father and co-dependent mother. Her tears had slayed me, but she told me I shouldn't feel sorry. I had to live my own life. And for her, our father had been indifferent. He hadn't seen her as a threat. Trying to figure out why he was so hard on me was useless since we'd never get any answers. He'd gone to his grave holding onto a bottle of cheap bourbon and plenty of secrets.

Working through our shared memories about a man who was afraid to fail and never took any chances in bettering himself probably had more to do with his own upbringing than any shortcomings he constantly railed about where I was concerned. He had an excuse for everything and a solution for nothing.

The longer the night wore on, the more I came to realize that my father, for all his many faults, had needed exactly what he denied me. Love and understanding toward me as an individual. It was one of those ah-ha moments I remember overhearing on a TV program my mom loved to watch when I was a teenager.

I ended up telling Evie how I handled seeing our old house with Scarlett and Matty in the car. In fact, I told her a lot about Scarlett and as I went on, her eyes grew wider and wider. "Hold it. You've been back in town how long? Do you hear how you're talking about this woman, Cole? I'm thinking you need to go over to her house right now, wake her up if you have to and apologize for being a horse's ass. Sounds like maybe I'm not the only one who's found that special someone."

When I didn't argue, she got weepy, then she stood up from the table in the restaurant where we'd been for hours; the wait staff were on the verge of kicking us out anyway. "Go. Now. I don't care how late it is. She needs to know how you feel about her. And I need to get home to Sam."

I always knew my sister was the smarter child.

"Cole? Do you know what time it is?"

Scarlett wore the same terry-cloth robe I first saw her in almost two weeks ago. Was I moving too fast? Actually, I felt like I wasn't moving fast enough. I mean, I never thought I'd find someone like her. Someone who could change my mind about commitment, and I wasn't willing to let her get away.

"Hi, yeah, it's uh, after eleven. I think. I thought you

might still be up studying, so I took a chance." I gave her a hopeful smile. My gut began to churn at the thought she'd refuse to speak with me.

But then relief flooded me as she stepped out onto the front porch, closing the door behind her. "Can this wait until tomorrow?" A piece of her thick auburn hair fell across her eyes and before she could, I brushed it away and tangled my hand in her thick locks, pulling her into me. I didn't ask. I just went for it.

I kissed her senseless. At least, that was my plan. She let out a low moan. Deepening the kiss, I poured my heart into it. Scarlett leaned in close, her hands on my chest.

"Wait!" She stepped back from me, her lips swollen hair mussed from my hands. "Just wait. What's going on with you? First you freeze me out for no apparent reason, now you want a booty call. Yeah, that's a hard no. Goodnight, Cole."

Hands sweaty, my heartbeat thrumming in my ears, I put my hand on the doorframe. I couldn't let her walk away, but I wasn't going to force her to listen if she didn't want to. Thinking fast, I let my true feelings rush out, no filter.

"I didn't think I'd find anything in Pineville except bitter memories and the random holiday with my sister. But you changed all that, Scarlett. You and Matty. I never thought I'd find something, someone worth opening my heart to, but now I can't imagine life without you in it. I didn't realize until now that I'd been waiting for you, baby." She froze, but didn't turn around. At least I had her attention. I pressed on.

"About earlier...what I should have told you was the neighborhood where Matty's friend lived. I grew up there. We passed my house, and I was so caught up in the moment with you, Matty...and my brain just locked up. I should have noticed the landmarks, but I was feeling a part of something bigger, you know? Something I hadn't gone looking for but thank the universe I found. Right next door to my sister."

Scarlett turned to face me, her expression unreadable, but it was enough to keep me going. To give me a shred of hope she'd forgive me.

"My dad treated me like crap. He drank. Every day that I can remember, he'd end it passed out in his recliner, at the kitchen table, and sometimes at the bar he stopped at after work. My mom would have to bundle us into the car to pick him up. He was a first-class son of a bitch. I couldn't wait to turn eighteen and leave home. I chose the Army and never looked back."

I wiped a tear from her cheek. "Aw, sweetheart. Don't cry. He's long gone, but I still let him take up space in my head. That's one of the reasons I'm here. Part of my recovery. After my injury, I began seeing a therapist to help with my PTSD and one of the things that came out was my anger toward my father. She suggested that since I couldn't talk to him, I come home and find a way to make peace because it was all intertwined with the guilt I was carrying over losing my men, my brothers-in-arms. And I blamed myself for their deaths. Made myself out to be the loser my dad had labeled me. And now I need to make sure that I don't repeat history. And that begins with an apology to the woman I love for not letting her in when I needed her the most."

Scarlett let out a small sob, then covered her mouth. I reached up and took her hands in mine, bringing them close to my heart.

"I love you, Scarlett. And I'm so sorry I pushed you away. I want to show you, and Matty, how special you are.

I'll be the best husband and father to your son, I promise. Please, forgive me?"

More tears streamed down her face, but I wasn't sure if she was happy, upset, or gearing up to curse me out.

"Oh my. For someone who says he's not good with words, that was perfect. And, yes! I love you too. I mean, I never thought I could love someone the way I love you. Or that I'd find a man who'd want both me and my son. You'd better be sure, Cole, because I will hold you to your promise. And I do forgive you." Scarlett kissed the lone tear that I couldn't hold back.

"Oh, I'm all in. And I know we haven't talked about this, but we better get married quick because I plan on getting you pregnant as soon as I can. I think Matty needs a sister or brother, don't you?"

I'd rendered her speechless and Scarlett's teary-eyed nod was all the answer I needed.

EPILOGUE

The following spring

WAITING TO MARRY SCARLETT HAD BEEN ONE OF THE hardest things I'd ever done, but I had to give away Evie first. Sam had proved to me he was the exact right guy for my sister. When I saw how he matched her wit and could hold his own without making her feel inferior, and how much he loved her, I knew she hadn't settled.

Scarlett and I waited until late spring to get married. My bride wanted an outdoor wedding and in north Idaho that meant waiting till at least mid-May. Besides, I couldn't say no to Scarlett. In fact, I planned on spending the rest of my life saying yes to her and our son, Matty. Well, almost my son. He'd surprised me during the ceremony. After I kissed Scarlett as we stood under an arch of her favorite flowers, pink peonies and red roses in the late evening sun, Matty handed me a large envelope. Its contents brought me to tears.

With Scarlett's blessing, he'd asked me to be his father.

Children may not have been on my radar, but there was nothing that would keep me from becoming his dad. My plan was to do the exact opposite of my own father. There would not be a day that went by that Matthew Oliver Nolan wouldn't feel safe, secure and, most of all, loved.

Evie, as her first act as Auntie, kept Matty with her and Sam while we went on our honeymoon.

Scarlett had never been out of the US and had always wanted to visit France and Italy, so I surprised her with the trip of her dreams.

Today was our fourth night in Paris and tomorrow we'd be leaving for Venice. While she changed for dinner, I stepped out onto the balcony off our suite and marveled at where I was and how I got here.

It didn't last long. My cell went off and, for a moment, panic hit me. Everyone in our lives knew we were on our honeymoon and wouldn't dare interrupt, so in my mind, that meant something bad had happened.

It was a text from Beckett. I let out a breath I hadn't realized I'd been holding.

He'd made his retirement official and wanted to let me know right away. Then he told me to get back to my, hopefully, naked wife. I shook my head and laughed. Maybe seeing how happy I was with Scarlett would change his mind about women.

During my bachelor party, which had turned out to be a steak dinner with just him and Sam, we'd discussed a conversation from years ago when we were dug in, taking heavy fire from the Taliban. During a lull in the early hours before dawn, we talked about what our dream job would be once we were out of the military. It took our minds off the debilitating heat and the constant threat of death.

Beck had grown up close to his carpenter dad and, at

one point, had thought he'd follow in his footsteps. But when he hit his senior year, he decided he wanted to get out of his tiny hometown in southern Texas. We'd made somewhat of a loose pact that if we both got out of Afghanistan alive and after our time in the Army was up, we'd go into business together. He'd teach me the techniques his dad had passed along to him as a finish carpenter and I'd handle the paperwork, scheduling, and so on.

But now that I had a family, becoming my own boss would have to wait. Once we returned from our honeymoon, I would start working for Carter Security. Sam had recommended me to the owner, who happened to be a close friend of his. They provided security for the Idaho Outlaws as well as other large businesses in Pineville.

I'd wait and see what Beck decided. If he did end up in Pineville, then I could feel him out and see what his plans were. And who knows, maybe he'd find someone almost as perfect as Scarlett.

For now, my priority was Scarlett, Matty, and after this honeymoon, hopefully, we'd be expecting a baby. Lord knows I'd given it my all in that department this past week.

At the thought of how we'd been doing our best to get her pregnant, my cock hardened, remembering all the interesting positions we'd tried. In fact, I looked around the balcony and thought maybe I could convince her to give outdoor sex a try. After the sun went down, of course.

"Cole?" Scarlett's voice carried outside to me, but when she didn't appear, I walked back inside to our suite's living room, but it was empty. So I went into the bedroom, where I noticed the door to the bathroom stood open. Inside, I found her standing next to the sink, a look of awe on her face. She was holding a white stick.

"That what I think it is?"

Her face split into a huge grin. She launched herself at me, wrapping her arms around my neck and her legs around my waist.

"Two pink lines." The joy in her voice pulled a laugh cry combo out of me and I swung her around, captured her mouth before she could say anything else, and carried her into the bedroom, placing her gently on the comforter. She wore only a slip, which made it easy to get her the rest of the way naked.

Scarlett placed a hand on my chest when I leaned over her. "You know, now that we know I'm pregnant, we don't have to keep trying so much. We can go back to the...uh, regular amount of sex."

I took her hand off my chest and kissed her palm. "Oh, my love, but we do unless, wait, are you not feeling well? Are you queasy? Can I get you anything?" My heart raced. Worry for her and our baby filled me. *Our baby. Hot damn.*

Scarlett reached up, pulling me back toward her. She took my right hand and placed it over her lower belly. "Our little peanut isn't even the size of a peanut yet. We have plenty of time before I'm anywhere close to not wanting you and I hardly had any morning sickness with Matty, so maybe I'll get lucky there, too."

But the more I think about it, we probably should have as much sex as possible before we go home. We'll be busy with our soon-to-be six-year-old, then there's your new job, my job and day sex will be but a fond memory."

Oh, I loved this woman. "Well, when you put it that way, Mrs. Nolan. I think we'll be ordering room service tonight...tomorrow morning, and until our flight home."

"That, Mr. Nolan, is an excellent plan."

TANGLING WITH THE PLAYER

Thea Lynch

I'm not sure what made me do it.

The devil? *Too easy*.

My boss? *Maybe*.

My screaming libido? *Ding, ding, ding—we have a winner*.

Winning a dinner date with the hunky baseball player at the charity auction hadn't been my intention. My boss dared me.

My family and friends constantly tell me I need to lighten up—I'm too serious, career driven, and they say I scare men away. *Whatever*.

But there's something about *him* and a dare's a dare, right?

He promises to keep his hands to himself, but do I want to hold him to his promise or ask him to show to me what it's like to be desired by the league's hottest player?

Brock Cameron

It's my last year in the league and the PR department talks me into a bachelor auction. It's for my favorite charity so I dust off my tux and play the role that's unfairly followed me my entire career—playboy athlete.

She's the opposite of my usual type. She has brains AND beauty.

She's a little grumpy, but nothing I can't handle.

Besides, once I sit across from her, I can't stop thinking how she'd taste and look after a night spent in my bed.

Thinking fast because I can't let her walk away, I tell her I could use some help with upcoming social events and ask her to be my fake girlfriend. Incredibly, she agrees.

I suspect she sees right through my lame attempts at impressing her, but I'm determined to put some sunshine into her life, chasing away her grumpy façade on the way to my first and last happily ever-after.

CHAPTER ONE

THEA

"Thea Lynch, this is absolutely the craziest thing you've ever done." I whisper the words to myself as I make my way through the crowded ballroom, avoiding eye contact with anyone I know.

Unfortunately, almost everyone I know is in the room. Well, almost everyone excluding my older brother, Colton, who was out of town. My younger sister, Brenley, who had supplied the gorgeous floral centerpieces from her new floral shop, was somewhere in the room and probably laughing her ass off.

I nodded at acquaintances and several people I met through my job, when the sudden and sad realization that I didn't have friends outside of work or whom I hadn't met through work smacked me in the face.

So, yeah, everyone outside of family was here to witness my ramped up yet thoroughly under-used libido. And maybe I caved to the pressure of my boss' teasing, along with her all-star player husband. They'd dared me a few days ago to help them out at the celebrity bachelor charity auction the Outlaws were a major sponsor of and had two members of the team participating.

And I just won a fantasy date with the Playboy Player. The "hard body of hard ball", the man who otherwise would never look twice at me.

Refusing to appear embarrassed, desperate, or worse, giddy at the prospect of going on a date with one of the hottest baseball players in the country, I bypassed the stage. I was not going to follow in the footsteps of the previous winners who'd fawned all over their "dates."

Instead, I'd kept my cool, keeping my face neutral when the auctioneer declared me the winner. I made a beeline for the exit and, as much as my high heels allowed me to, I quickly made my way out of the ballroom, then down the hallway where the checkout area was located for the winners to pay. *What had I been thinking?* This was so unlike me. And I couldn't even blame it on too much champagne. I'd agreed to this, but the reality of it brought all my younger self's insecurities bubbling to the surface.

Passing life sized photos of all the bachelors lined along the walls, I came face to face with the high-resolution print of my date. I stumbled slightly at the intensity of his light hazel eyes peering back at me. Brock Cameron, third baseman for the Idaho Outlaws, notorious playboy and Pineville's favorite hometown boy, had risen to fame and fortune with his on-the-field talent and the league's highest batting average year after year.

He made my heart skip, my lady bits tingle and question my sanity. The first two I could hide. But the last one? It was on full display earlier as I raised the paddle handed to me by my boss, Kelsey Jansen, with the assurance her husband, Maverick, and star pitcher for the Idaho Outlaws, would pay the winning bid. It was for a good cause, after all. All the funds raised tonight would go to the local club for disadvantaged youth, The Children's Club, and other charities in the Pineville area.

"Thea, wait!?" My boss' voice rang out. Kelsey caught up to me, cradling her very pregnant belly.

My stomach dropped at the sight. I fast walked back to her. "Kelsey, are you crazy? Slow down or that baby is going to make an unscheduled appearance, and I'm not taking the blame when Mav finds out you were running down the hall after me." My hands were outstretched in a vain attempt to keep said baby from hitting the ground should my thoughts become reality.

"Stop worrying about me. I'm just here to pay." She sidestepped me, waving what I could only assume was Mav's black Amex card, and stepped up to the alcove where the event's staff was taking payment. She signed the receipt, then turned back to me. Just watching her made me dizzy.

"Kelsey, this is insane. I can't believe I listened to you and Mav. Maybe it's not too late and we can go speak with the lady who lost? I'm sure she'd be *ecstatic* to go on the date with Brock."

Yes, I knew better than to talk my boss out of anything, let alone her and Mav's screwy attempt at match-making, but the swarm of butterflies in my gut made me try.

"This is not going to work, Kels. I don't know what I was thinking. Because obviously I was not thinking. And I can't even blame it on alcohol since I agreed to do this two days ago!"

"What are you really worried about, Thea? This is exactly what you need. You are way too serious about everything and don't pull that face with me. I'm worried about you. So, sue me. You need to loosen up, have some fun. What better way than a night out with the handsome Brock Cameron?"

She was making me sound like I never had any fun. Well, so what if I preferred a quiet night in rather than clubbing? My friends were constantly trying to set me up, and I was constantly shooting them down. Not that I didn't want a man in my life, I just wanted the right man. And he wouldn't be found in a bar, online or at a bachelor auction, of *that* I was sure.

But as soon as I had the thought, a part of me screamed *"Liar, liar, pants on fire."* If there was one man who could make me change my mind, it was Brock.

How Kelsey and Maverick knew I had a secret thing for the six-foot-two chiseled ballplayer, I had no idea, and for once I know I should stop being a "negative Nelly" and go with the flow but old habits were hard to break. My sister long ago labeled me a grump, and it stuck. I didn't think I was a grumpy person. Guarded and skeptical of people's motivations? Of men in general? Sure. Our parents' screwed up relationship had sent me down that path where Brenley had chosen to go in the opposite direction. I loved her to death, but her constant cheery outlook would make anyone else seem a bit grumpy.

Pushing aside my brooding thoughts, I said, "Let's get you back to your table so you can sit down." Turning on a ridiculously high heel, I smacked into a wall. A firm, muscular wall encased in a custom midnight blue tux.

"Brock, perfect timing. This is Thea Lynch. Thea, Brock Cameron." Kelsey stood next to us, beaming like a proud mother, oblivious to my instant embarrassment.

Reeling from the contact with Brock's chest, I took a moment to catch my breath. Leaning back, I smiled, or gave it my best shot, then nodded and tried to untangle myself from him.

But Brock wasn't letting go. He had a large hand on my shoulder and the other around my waist as he steadied us both, and I had to fight from melting into his warmth. A quick inhale had me taking in his spicy cologne mingled with his unique musk. It had all my nerve endings firing and my girly parts singing, "*Oh, my*."

"You okay, Thea? Sorry. This wasn't the way I wanted to meet." His smile lit up his face.

My eyes zeroed in on his full lips as they spread wide. Fighting my body's reaction, I tried to keep my features neutral, only giving him the tiniest of smiles in return.

There was no way I was going to let him know how much his presence, his touch, affected me. It was a knee jerk reaction I used whenever I found myself with a man who I was attracted to. Something I'd perfected in college, when I'd been shot down in spectacular fashion by the big man on campus in front of all my friends.

Some things you just never forget.

I hadn't been thin enough, or pretty enough, for him and he'd let me know…loudly, and even though he'd been inebriated, and my friends tried to convince me it was no big deal, I knew the truth. There was an old saying, "A drunk man's words are a sober man's thoughts," and it launched me into a panic attack that from that moment on had me surrounding myself with a heavily guarded wall on my emotions whenever I found myself attracted to a man.

And man was I attracted to Brock. In fact, it went way beyond attraction. I was so turned on by him right now I feared he could sense it and use it against me somehow.

So, I held myself stiff, but not quickly enough. My body had already settled into his frame when my hands had grabbed onto his broad shoulders. And, oh how those shoulders felt under my sweaty palms as I dug into his hard flesh through the silky material of his tux.

When it dawned on me that I had a death grip on him, I leaned back so I could put much needed distance between us, but his arm tightened, keeping me from moving away.

And there we were, locked in an intimate embrace for maybe less than five seconds, but it was the best five seconds ever. And my body had a mind of its own. My soft curves pressed up against his hard, muscled frame was heaven itself and what I imagined the feeling of instant connection would be. But it was simply wishful thinking.

Swallowing a low moan, I quickly schooled my features, flattened my hands on his chest, and pushed away. I could have wept from the loss of contact and the heat I'd absorbed from him. A chill swept over me, almost like my body was mocking me for giving up so soon on the bliss I felt in his arms. My head was swirling, and I wanted to lean forward and bury my nose in the crook of his neck and take another hit of his addicting scent. But I kept it together, falling back on my years-long perfected persona of being unaffected, disinterested and slightly annoyed by someone who dared showed me the tiniest bit of interest.

Yeah, I know how eff'd up that sounds, but after the humiliation in college plus years of seeing my mother deal with a cold, emotional closed off husband who never showed her the physical affection she craved, I'd developed what I thought was a failsafe solution to avoid any hint of rejection by a man.

But for a moment, that one perfect moment, I was almost positive I read interest, maybe even desire, in his eyes as I broke out of his hold before I allowed insecurity to take the reins once again. I nodded coolly, then mumbled something I wouldn't remember later even if offered a million dollars and excused myself.

Striding toward the ladies' room, I heard Kelsey apologize for me. Disappointment laced her tone, loud and clear. I berated myself for messing things up for her and Mav. Then, right before I entered the ladies' room, I looked back. Why I tortured myself I couldn't say, but I felt as if they'd been watching me flee and I just had to see if the itch of mutual desire I'd felt in his arms was real.

A shiver ran through me at seeing Brock's gaze locked on me. Not in anger at my obvious rudeness, but something I hadn't dared thought could be possible. His gaze was loaded with heat as it roamed over me and finally settling on my face. One corner of his mouth lifted, and I swore he was daring me to call him out for the obvious full-body scan that left me flushed and needy.

Instead, I did what I always did. I ignored it and him, bolting into the washroom.

Standing in front of the long row of sinks and mirrors, I braced my hands on the cool granite and stared at my wild-eyed reflection.

What the hell is wrong with me?

CHAPTER TWO

BROCK

I hadn't anticipated the excitement over having the curvy brunette being the highest bidder. And even though the brief and puzzling interaction with Thea left me curious at her reaction, I was turned on, no electrified by her body running into mine. The experience giving me an immediate thrill of possibility I don't ever remember feeling toward a woman.

Maverick had been on my case for the last year once I confided in him about my plans. I was ready to retire after one more season. He told me it was time to find "the one" and start a family, leaving my playboy image behind. It was an image that may have been true the first few years of my career, but I had left that lifestyle long ago; unfortunately, the media hadn't.

So, ever since he married Kelsey, Mav had become the poster boy for marriage and family life. They were expecting their second kid, and he'd become more annoying than ever.

But he was right, I just wasn't going to tell him that, yet.

I'd always wanted the same thing. I just hadn't found the right woman despite the reputation the press had built up for me, that the only playing the field I did was on the baseball diamond.

Not that I'd been a monk, but I was choosy about who I dated, who I slept with. Most of the women I was pictured with I'd only taken out once for an event or a dinner date or two. I didn't want to waste my time and, more importantly, their time on something that wasn't going anywhere.

I'd learned at an early age what a happy relationship and a solid marriage looked like. My parents were still going strong after close to forty years, and I wasn't going to settle for anything less than what they had. My father claimed it was instant love for him when he met my mom, and I guess I'd always thought the same would happen to me.

Now, with one more year left in the United States Baseball League, I was determined to find her. I had viewed tonight's auction as the jumping off point for my search. And as much as my free time allowed, I was going to find her. Someone who was comfortable in the spotlight since my plan was to remain tied to the league in some way, either in coaching or broadcasting, because I wasn't ready to completely walk away from the sport I loved.

I felt she was out there, somewhere. It may take some time to find her, but I'm a determined man when I put my mind to a project. The future Mrs. Cameron had to like baseball, working with the community, want to have kids, love cats, be adventurous…and be able to put up with me. I've been described as overly optimistic, which I don't get why that would be seen as a mark against me, but I know sometimes I can be too Miss Mary Sunshine in a career filled with testosterone fueled alpha males, but that's me.

Like me or not, I've decided to live my life seeking the sun, not avoiding the storm.

Part of that credit had to go to my notorious grump of a grandfather. He showed me what I *didn't* want to be. My father's father woke up on the wrong side of the bed every day. At eleven years old, I made a conscience decision to *not* be like my namesake. And when he died at sixty-two, I knew, just knew, that I needed to live life to the max, every…single…day.

And the woman who I give my heart to needed to understand that or she wouldn't be the one for me.

"Hey, Brock. Over here, man." Maverick's voice carried over the loud din of the ballroom as I made my way back to my table.

"How do you feel? You good?"

I accepted a couple high fives from my teammates. "Alright, settle down. What are you, twelve?"

"She's hot, Cameron. You so lucked out. There was a seventy-something lady waving that paddle like a pom-pom towards the end of the bidding."

"Did you see the swing of her hips? Man, your drought is over. But if she decides she needs a younger guy, give her my number and I'll make sure she gets her thirst quenched." Brett King, the Outlaw's twenty-three-year-old rookie, razzed me.

Maverick cuffed Brett on the back of the head as I took my seat and let the smack-talk slide right off. "Guys, settle down. It's for charity. This is not about hooking up, okay? It's merely a bonus that the woman who won the bid is pretty. Now let's settle down and pay attention. Ace is up next." I was still processing the few moments I had with

Thea, and I wasn't ready to share my feelings with my teammates.

The Outlaw's pitching coach, Ace Jefferson, took the stage and a couple wolf whistles followed him down the runway as the bidding began. He'd been divorced for a couple years and thanks to a viral picture of him in a local gym working out without a shirt on, he'd become famous for more than his coaching skills. At forty-two, he was now dealing with women sliding into his DMs or approaching him in the grocery store and fawning all over him.

I enjoyed giving him a hard time over it, because now I wasn't the only single guy on the team the media followed, picking apart our dating life.

Maverick clapped a hand on my shoulder and raised his voice to be heard over the emcee, encouraging the bidders. "Thanks again for agreeing to the auction. I know you and Thea will hit it off."

Only myself, Mav and his wife Kelsey, and Thea, knew that no matter how high the bidding went, the Jansen's were footing the bill. For whatever reason, they thought tonight and our "date" would help me out with TMZ's obsession in linking me up to every young starlet or pop singer who happened to attend an Outlaw game or after-party.

Heck, I rarely attended any of the home game after parties thrown at the Outlaws' favorite hangout, a dinner and dance club owned by their outfielder, Connor Holt's wife. So, when I made an appearance a couple weeks ago when it was Connor's birthday, photos were snapped of me standing next to a girl I didn't even know.

My world had blown up with constant speculation and photographers camped outside my house. If this kept up once the season started, it was going to collide with the team's owner and the front office's plans for my farewell season. And so, the plan was quietly hatched to find a distraction. It would be a short-term solution that Kelsey assured me would work. And hopefully the media would move on to the next "it" couple.

I was adamant about not pretending to date anyone. That wasn't fair to the woman or me, and I squashed that idea right away. But I wasn't opposed to taking control of my public persona and beating the media at their own game. And if during the process I found the woman I want to spend the rest of my life, all the better. Because seeing how happy Mav and my other recently married teammates were had sparked enough envy within me to make it happen.

Tuning everyone around me out, my thoughts were full of Thea and wanting to see her again…soon. Fate, it seemed, was definitely and finally on my side. And if my body's response to her was anything to go by, I was well on my way to finding the one.

CHAPTER THREE

THEA

Kelsey waddled over to my desk, slowly sat down in the brown leather club chair, and rubbed her belly. "It's been three days, Thea. Why haven't you set up your date with Brock yet?"

I ignored the exasperation laced in her voice and pointed my pen at her movements. "Why haven't you gone home yet? You're less than a week away from your due date. Second baby's come quicker. Or so I hear."

Kelsey snorted and shifted. I felt the wince on her face as if I was carrying the baby. A twinge of jealousy hit me. I was not a jealous person. Nor would anyone label me sentimental. But damn if my upcoming thirty-fifth birthday hadn't caused a new level of anxiety I hadn't anticipated.

There weren't many times I questioned my decision to start a family of my own when I was younger, but the last few weeks of her pregnancy had sparked a teeny bit of wistfulness. Especially when her handsome hubby was around making sure she took care of herself and then when I saw him with Mari, their two-year-old, forget it. The cuteness gripped and squeezed my heart, and my eggs may have rattled a time or two when he walked into the offices with his daughter's arms wrapped around his neck.

"Thea." Kelsey had the mom tone down and she aimed it directly at me. Sighing, I turned from the computer screen and gave her my full attention. "Well, *Mom*. I've been giving that some thought."

"You mean you've developed cold feet, right?"

Kelsey didn't push further than that. She knew my backstory. Why I was still single and a non-believer in happily ever after. Sure, I've seen it work for some of my friends, but I'd grown up in a home with an unemotional father who'd driven my mother to drink. Why she never left him had haunted me and colored my view on relationships forever. Maybe if she'd left, found someone else to give her, show her the love she so desperately craved, then maybe my outlook would be different.

But she didn't.

And I would forever have those memories, the flashbacks to their fights when he'd tell her he was who he was, and she married him, so don't ask for change because it wasn't going to happen. I shook the horror of seeing my mother wither away, feeling unloved in a sexless marriage. She died from cancer five years ago and I hadn't spoken or seen my father since.

I couldn't speak for my siblings, but burying the grief and putting all my energy into my career were the only things that had kept me sane.

Even though I've never had a long-term relationship, that didn't mean I didn't date. I enjoyed sex too much to cut myself off from men entirely.

I was just picky.

And typically, my friends never knew the guy. So going on a date with the sinfully hot Brock Cameron would break *all* the rules I had set for myself a very long time ago. Agreeing to bid on him during the charity auction so he wasn't saddled with what the media had affectionately coined, "Brock's Bunnies", made me want to throw up, but I also understood how he had nothing to do with how women reacted to him. I got a full dose the other night and my body still perked up at the memory.

Yeah, I'd let my desire to be a team player overrule all my...rules. Ugh, and okay, so my long-ignored libido had gone along and I blamed it as the reason behind raising my hand and offering myself as tribute before my good sense had a chance to kick in.

When Kelsey had pointed out a recent headline piggybacking on the fervor over his upcoming retirement: "Wife Watch: Who will land the Playboy Player?" I found it wholly unfair. No one should have their decision to not marry questioned. She knew that would get me to agree, but now I was second-guessing this date.

"Okay, I get the whole public aspect of going out with Brock. Get the media off his back and make it easier for him to focus on his job and helping the Outlaws get back into the championship series, but--"

Kelsey interrupted my swirling thoughts and held up her free hand while continuing to rub the side of her belly with the other.

"No buts and no excuses. I need you to follow through on the date. The charity has received the donation and now the date needs to happen. In a month, he can't afford any questions about why the date hasn't happened. Brock is expecting your call. There's just a month and a half before the start of spring training, Thea."

A small wave of nausea shot into the pit of my stomach. Not because of going on the date, but who it was with. Because what girl wouldn't want to be treated to a night of luxury at the lake resort, being waited on and eating food created by a three Michelin star chef? Not to mention having the undivided attention of a handsome man. Any woman over eighteen would give her favorite pair of heels to spend thirty minutes with not just Pineville's, but the sports world's most eligible bachelor.

Why couldn't I just be like my single girlfriend's and be blissfully excited about this opportunity or even love? Not that I expected to fall in love after one date. In my opinion, insta love only happened in fairy tales and romance books.

But what if Brock likes you? Isn't keeping up that wall exhausting? Ugh, sometimes I hated my inner self.

"Okay. Soon, I promise." Throwing my hands up in defeat, I knew Kelsey wasn't going to let me off the hook, so I gave in to the inevitable.

What could it hurt to indulge in one night of fantasy, even if he was a notorious player?

CHAPTER FOUR

BROCK

Five days. It had been almost a whole week, and I hadn't received an email, a phone call. Hell, even a measly text to arrange the date she'd won. Okay, been set up to win, but still. I'd left two voicemails for Thea at her work. Maybe she was sick? I needed to find out what was going on. The local newspaper had reached out and asked if they could send a photographer along on our "date" and I'd debated.

If I said no, they'd probably stake out my house and follow me. If I said yes, it would go a long way in getting the press off my back about my private life. Either way, it would suck. I put them off because I was embarrassed to admit that the woman who'd won had been avoiding my calls.

In less than six weeks, pitchers and catchers reported to begin training, and I wanted no distractions during my final year. And Thea Lynch was quickly becoming a distraction, and I'd only met her once. My body's instant connection when I had her curvy body in my arms had been fueling my dreams and my growing anticipation for our date.

Thea was my favorite type of woman. Smart. Curvy. Not too short, not too tall. Long hair I can wrap my hand around to tug and angle her full, pouty lips to the perfect height for me to sip and lick and…yeah, I got all that during our brief moment in the hallway with Kelsey observing.

It hadn't mattered who was there or how many people passed us in those few short minutes. For the first time in my life, I was captivated by a woman.

Thea, on the other hand, seemed polite at best and at worst more than slightly unimpressed by me. In the days since, listening to her outgoing message laced with her cool demeanor had me wanting to find out what made her tick. Why did she agree to bid on me and then act as if she was disappointed or no longer interested once we met?

She was an unexpected challenge I couldn't wait to see again.

My fingers itched to touch her again to see if what I felt had been my imagination or caught up in a moment or was simply horny. Hell, maybe it was a combination of all three. Either way, I was going to get that date scheduled.

And the surest way of gaining a woman's attention was to give her no choice.

~

After contacting the local newspaper and arranging for one of their photographers to meet me at the team's headquarters, I called Kelsey to give her a heads up on my plans. I wanted to ensure Thea was in her office when I showed up.

Flowers in hand, I stepped off the elevator at the Idaho

Outlaws front office. Attached to the baseball stadium affectionately labeled The Glass Cathedral by the locals was where the club's management and staff worked pretty much year round. Kelsey had assured me Thea was still there.

Stepping off the elevator, Lois, Thomas Scott's executive assistant, was waiting for me. "Hello, Brock. Thea's still in the conference room. They just wrapped up a meeting. Did you want to do this stunt in there or wait till she's back in her office?"

I blinked at Lois' statement, then let out a chuckle. "I'm up for either, Mrs. Campbell. I understand you think this might not go over well with Thea, but I prefer to look on the positive side."

TS' long time right hand, a woman he considered family and one I did not want to cross, returned his smile. "My money's on you. But it's not going to be easy. She's a tough cookie, so be prepared."

The photographer piped up, "Is anyone else in the room with her?"

The man was fairly vibrating with excitement over the opportunity to be inside the Outlaw's inner sanctum. I'd had to promise Kelsey I wouldn't make Thea feel uncomfortable or cornered and keep the guy in check.

It wasn't a hard promise to make. My goal was to get some face time with the beauty who had me tied up in knots.

Turning to the photographer, I gave him my best glare. "Remember the deal, Peter. Only pictures of me with Thea. Got it?"

"Yeah, yeah. Don't worry. I'm aware of the rules."

A movement down the hall caught my eye, and I forgot about the over eager photog. Thea exited the conference room. She was walking in the opposite direction and hadn't noticed me.

But I'd sure noticed her.

And the swing of her hips.

Hips encased in a curve-hugging navy skirt topped with a white blouse cinched at her waist by a wide leather belt. I easily imagined myself capturing those curves in my hands and pulling her against me. Her hair was loosely captured up in a twist, begging to be tugged free. Burying my hands in her thick locks to hold her still as I devoured her full lips became the dominant need and as soon as I had her alone, my top priority.

"Brock?"

Kelsey's voice cut through my desire-filled fog. I snapped my attention back to her and turned to see a knowing smirk plastered on the VP of Communications' face. "You can't ask her to dinner if you stand there. Get a move on Cameron." Kelsey ducked into her office, soft laughter echoing off the tiled floors.

Grinning, I cleared my throat, adjusted my tie, and moved swiftly down the long hallway. A feeling of anticipation that I was walking toward a life-altering moment. I hadn't felt this since I was drafted into the USBL. Surrounded by family, I'd floated for a week after receiving *the* call. This felt the same. With an added megadose of electricity.

Thea's door was open, and she was busily tapping away on her keyboard. I held the flowers I made sure were her favorites in front of me, knocked on the door, leaned against the doorframe and waited for her to look up.

"Yes, that works for us. I'll run it by the player union's and get back to you." Thea punched a button on her desk phone, then ran both her hands over her face. "Sometimes I fear for humanity."

A soft growl laced her words, and I couldn't hold in my chuckle. She jumped at the sound, letting out the cutest squeak. I angled my body closer, blocking the jittery photographer behind me who I now cursed for being witness to what should have been a private moment.

I scrambled for something to say that would get her to smile. To take a chance on the spark that ignited a week ago.

"I don't fear so much as hope for the best. I honestly think most people need a good hug. Or some of my sister Holly's famous lemon shortbread on a Sunday afternoon spent recharging."

Thea's eyes narrowed where another woman's might have gone wide and her lips pinched together, where other's might curve up. Her posture snapped straight, on high alert when the goal had been to have her lean in toward me and share a moment of humor.

I had my work cut out for me. But in the end, would it be worth it? Man, I hoped so.

Smiling, I waited.

"And who am I supposed to be in that scenario?" She asked.

Never let them see you sweat. Most importantly, the woman whose lips I desperately wanted to taste before the day ended. "Miss Thea, you are unlike any other 'people' I've ever had the pleasure of meeting. And I'm here to take you on our date." I handed her the flowers and stepped aside so Peter could begin snapping pictures.

A muffled snort emitted from behind me. Damn, photographer.

"Hey, man, whose side are you on?" I shifted, speaking

out of the side of my mouth toward my least favorite person at the moment.

"Who else is out there?" Thea leaned to the side, craning her neck to look behind me. Things weren't quite going the way I'd envisioned in my head. I used visualization often when I played. A technique I relied upon heavily when I stepped into the batter's box and had great success with based on my lifetime stats for both RBIs and hits.

Thea's movement had me moving on the fly to offer my hand as she stood, pulling her close and placing the large bouquet in her hands. "Smile, beautiful, I'll make this up to you, promise."

Her eyebrows shot up at my request, but Thea was a professional and she played along. And miracle of miracles, her lips curved up instead of down and her lovely eyes locked onto mine.

Was it weird that I sensed it was offered with great reluctance and that she probably would rather kick me in my shin? Definitely. But that was why I was here. Why I was pursuing her like I had no other woman. If any of my teammates could see how hard I was working to convince this suspicious woman...no, guarded fit her better, then I'd be spending my last year in the big leagues being razzed to no end.

But in my gut, in my heart, and yeah, ok I'm a guy so, in my pants—I knew *she* was worth all my efforts. There was just something about Thea Lynch that pulled me in, even though she'd done her best to push me away.

"Hold it...right there...and perfect. That's the shot." Peter fiddled with his camera, then aimed it back toward us. "Brock, could you turn toward me and put your arm around Thea's shoulders?"

"No," I answered. I didn't want to turn away. I wanted

to stay right where I was and absorb her reaction to me before she realized what was happening and hide her feelings from me like she did the night we met.

I noticed a flash of interest when I shot down the photographer and instead kept my gaze locked on her. Then her lips. She was nervous. I could feel her shiver. She licked her lips, and it took all I had to suppress a moan and from leaning down and tasting her.

"I just want one more picture, then I'll be on my way and meet you at the resort."

And there went the moment. It was like a gate slamming shut and Thea turned all business, no play. Eyes narrowing toward the not so patient Peter, she stepped back from me. Instantly I felt cool air rush in to replace the warmth of her body that had all too briefly been fueling mine.

"The resort? As in the Resort on the Lake, resort?"

Her eyes widened. One hand went to her hip as she gripped the flowers in the other. Thea's lips were shaped in a plump pout, one I wanted to rub my thumb over until they widened just enough so I could wipe away her frown.

"Brock?"

I cleared my throat and my thoughts. "Um, yeah?" I fought the urge to gather her in my arms and put my thoughts into action. Because her first reaction, a flash of desire flickering in her eyes when I touched her, was the one I was going to believe. And now it was as if she was purposely holding back her true feelings. I was determined to reignite the flame.

"Right. The resort. I have a dinner reservation set up." Glancing at my watch, I grinned. "And I have a limo waiting to take us there now. I already checked with Kelsey, so I know you don't have to work late or have anything else planned." Holding out my arm, "Shall we go?" The combined waver and huskiness of my voice took me by surprise. Maybe I wasn't as confident as I was trying to portray. Would she shoot me down?

Thankfully, she saved me from looking like a loser in front of Peter and, more importantly, Lois and Kelsey. Thea grabbed her handbag and waved her hand toward me. "Sure, lead the way."

It wasn't the excited response I was hoping for, but I'd take it.

CHAPTER FIVE

THEA

Seated in the back of the limo on the short ride over to The Resort on the Lake, his thigh brushed mine. The back of his warm, sun-kissed hand bumped mine when he handed me a glass of champagne. On the ride up in the hotel's elevator to the top floor where the restaurant was located, our fingers accidentally brushed twice. It was more action than I'd had in months. I lost count the number of times I squeezed my thighs together.

I had to admit that in all my dating life, this was a first for me. The man, the venue, lit up like a big announcement or proposal was about to happen. The tiniest of cracks appeared in my fortified wall.

Not one to be dazzled by much, Brock had me looking forward to the evening. I followed the hostess, and Brock followed me. Close enough, I could feel his body heat the entire way as we were led toward the floor to ceiling windows and a secluded corner lit up with candles.

Brock's hand brushed my elbow, guiding me to my seat, and I gritted my teeth at yet another innocent touch. His body now close enough for me to take in another hit of his scent, absorbing the tingles created by his hot breath near my ear as he spoke.

"We have the place to ourselves for an hour. It's the best I could do on short notice. But it will give us a chance to talk uninterrupted."

He remained at my side, patiently waiting until I settled. I peeked up at him and quickly became lost in his smile. A smile that reached his eyes. His laugh lines fanning out to his temples where hints of silver threaded through his black hair added to instead of detracting from his handsome face.

The moment sparked a secret thrill within me. His closeness made me forget, if for a moment, that this date wasn't real. Then the over eager photographer broke the spell.

"That's great, Brock. How about a kiss on the cheek? Our readers will eat this up." Pete the sneak had appeared from nowhere, ruining the moment. I should thank him for his rudeness. It helped me remember this was all an illusion.

I just needed to remind my libido and maybe I could make it through the dinner without succumbing to Brock's charms because if ever there was a man who could make me forget my carefully fortified wall of protection, then it was the sexy player in front of me who tactfully sent the annoying photographer on his way.

"Sorry about that. I know you understand because, well, you agreed to the auction thing, but now that we have that out of the way, what would you like to drink? Wine, a cocktail?"

Brock had taken his seat and was looking at the wine

menu, the sommelier standing at his side, both men looking at me expectantly.

If ever there was a time I should order an entire bottle just for myself, it was now. But my sister's scolding face appeared in my head, reminding me that I needed to give tonight a shot. I'd texted her during the short limo ride, asking her to call and give me an out. Make up some type of emergency. But she refused and said she hoped I would get lucky with the player.

Yeah, like that was going to happen. Besides, Brock was the opposite of my type. I typically went for the introverted, nerdy, good-looking but not too handsome guy instead of the hot, athletic, happily extroverted type that I pegged him for.

Just because I wasn't looking for happily ever after, didn't mean I didn't want a man in my bed. I just didn't want to live with a guy or be part of a couple.

I relaxed my face into a smile that hopefully didn't look forced and took the offered menu. Brock suggested we order our meal at the same time. I found one of my favorites and gave the sommelier my wine choice, along with my dinner order.

"I'll have the same." Brock's deep, husky baritone ignited warm fuzzies along my spine.

Oh man, I was in trouble.

"So, have you lived in Pineville long? I grew up here. I can't tell you how happy my parents were when the Outlaws relocated here." His question sounded so sincere, I almost answered. However, alarm bells went off. I didn't really want to spend the next hour exchanging in small talk or finding out about his personal life.

In what must have been a world record, our wine was presented, and the bottle was left in one of those fancy stands next to our table. I sent a smile and silent "thank you" to the fancy wine man and he gave me a discreet wink, then left as quickly as he'd appeared.

I took a fortifying sip of the excellent red bottled at a local winery and sighed. Time to set things straight. "We don't have to do this, you know. I'm good, I mean really good, with awkward silences as we enjoy our excellent meal and the view." I couldn't help myself. I smiled at Brock. His right eyebrow rose in that sexy way I'd seen only in movies, and I thawed another degree. This did not bode well for my imaginary wall.

"I'm getting the vibe that you don't put up with much, do you Thea?" Brock flashed me a panty-melting smile. I hated that cliché, but damn if it didn't fit him to a T.

"No. I tend to lean toward serious in-depth conversations about the state of the world or how we're not alone in the universe. Small talk gives me hives." After only a few of sips of wine, I felt myself relaxing, so I grinned back at him.

"Well, what if I told you I'm excellent at small talk, however I avoid anything political at all costs, and when I'm on the road, I binge watch whatever alien show or documentary I can find?" His dimple flashed before he took a sip of his wine.

My inner teen whimpered, then screamed in joy.

Good looks, intelligence, *and* he believes in aliens. Another crack threatened. I needed to clear my head. Otherwise, I was going to crumble when I needed to stand tall.

"Okay, I'll overlook your small talk skills. Tell me, how do you feel about reality TV? Your answer will serve as the tiebreaker. If you answer wisely, we can dive deep into the usual info dump shared during real first dates."

"Real? What about this?" Brock leaned back from the

table and swept his arm between us, then the room. "What about this isn't real? A shared bottle of wine, interesting conversation, and a beautiful woman. No matter how it was arranged, I consider this to be a real date. In fact, the more time I spend with you, the more I want to learn. There is something about you, Thea."

Beautiful? Now I knew he was only playing a part. For the press. For the public. But then the voice in my head whispered, *but what if he means what he says?*

My cell chimed. I'd forgotten to silence it. I grabbed it to change the setting, and a chime sounded from his phone. "Okay, that's not a coincidence, right?" I swiped the notification banner on my phone and was greeted with my face. And Brock's. Sitting at the table smiling at each other.

"What is it? You look like you've seen a ghost." Brock's concerned voice floated between us.

"Look at your phone. I wasn't expecting such a quick turnaround by the photographer." My hand shook while I stuffed my phone back into my purse. It was a good picture. Of both of us. And we looked good together.

"Nice picture. We look good together, don't you think?"

A weird cough escaped me at how closely his words echoed my thoughts. *Did he really think so?* His heated gaze locked on mine and suddenly, desperately, all I wanted to do was to lean forward, lick his full lips and beg him to kiss me breathless.

Catching myself as I began to do just that, I covered my movement by taking the napkin off the table, settling it upon my lap.

When I dared to look back up, Brock's eyebrows had risen. One corner of his mouth lifted, not in a smirk but in a swoon-worthy grin. And I—oh, how I wanted to believe him.

"Okay, back to your question. What if my answer is...unwise?"

His question broke the spell. I held my breath for three beats, then expelled it in three. A desperate attempt to calm my racing pulse, to shore up my defenses, keeping me immune from his charm assault.

"Being unwise will get you an hour of mindless commentary on the newest public relations strategies and how to increase a pro athlete's social media audience." Offering up the exact reason we were sitting across from the other would hopefully dissuade him from believing I could be easily charmed.

"Reality TV is the bane of our society. And I'm proud to say I've never watched a minute of a Kardashian, housewife or naked-something show. Game films and movies are my go-tos on any given night."

This time his words made me smile, a real smile I didn't have to force or wonder if it revealed too much of my feelings. My sister's constant reminder to enjoy the moments in my life without scrutiny or worry that I'd look silly popped into my head. She was right, but changing old habits was so hard.

If anyone could help me, the sexiest man I'd ever been on a fake date with just might be that man. Was I strong enough to let go and take Brenley's advice?

My emotions were all over the place. I was too young for my hormones to be failing me, although the thought of my upcoming birthday had me rethinking my current single status, but I was just old enough to know better than to think I have any real chance of catching Brock's interest. There was no way he'd choose me over his usual type: Perky thin women with big boobs. I cringed at my own cynical thoughts.

He was being nice. His only reason for surprising me at work and whisking me off to this fairy tale of a dinner was to fulfill his agreement and to throw off the media hounds who'd been creating nothing but headaches for him.

All I was to him was the willing woman who agreed to the dare thrown out by my boss and her husband during a long dry spell of no men and momentary insanity. I nudged my wineglass away. I would need a clear head to get through the rest of the evening.

"Have you been following me on social media? You couldn't have nailed the answer more perfectly." I lifted my water glass, toasting his successful response, then promptly drained the glass because the look he was giving me dried up every molecule of moisture in my body.

How was that even possible?

The man should come with a hazardous material warning.

"Why do you do that? It's like you don't believe me."

Luckily, I was rescued from coming up with another witty comeback. Our dinner arrived, and we dug into the perfectly prepared meal. Brock let the awkwardness of our previous conversation drop and peppered me with questions, and I answered them. We shared anecdotes from our childhood growing up in Pineville and the favorite places we both enjoyed. I glossed over my home life. There was no way I was going to share with him how my parents' dysfunctional relationship had formed my outlook on romantic relationships.

After we finished our dessert, he told me how he got back at TMZ for plastering a picture of him with a woman he never met all over the internet. It had me in stitches. "You did not send them a picture of your cat in a bikini. I call bullshit. You don't have a cat, do you?"

"It's true. And I do. My sister takes care of her when I'm on the road. And you have a wonderful laugh." Brock's unexpected compliment left me speechless. A condition I wasn't used to being in. Among my friends and family, I was more known for my lightning-quick responses, some said sarcastic or grumpy comebacks.

"You don't have to say that. It's fine."

"What are you talking about? Wait, do you have trouble taking compliments? My sister's the same way. But I mean it. I love your laugh."

Not the response I was expecting. "Please don't let the next words out of your mouth be: 'And you should laugh more.' Because if they are, I'd be forced to do something really stupid, like dump my drink in your lap."

Brock finished his wine and saluted me with his glass. "I think you're cautious, but I like that. It means you're not going to pretend to be someone you're not. There's a lot of fake people in this world and I've gotten pretty good at spotting them. You're real, at least from what I've seen so far tonight. So, please take it as it was meant to be. A compliment, nothing more."

Huh? I guess there was a first for everything. "Ok, well. Thank you. I...that's nice of you to say.

I leaned back in my seat and stared. Could I believe him? Why was I making such a big deal about him liking my laugh? I mean, I kind of liked my laugh too.

"Listen, I've been thinking. We seem to be getting along pretty well, and I know this was an unusual way to meet, but I have a proposition for you."

I felt my nipples go tight and my face warm at his words.

"Wait. No, that was a lame way to say it. I'm not hitting on you, not like that. Not that I don't think you're attractive and I would want you...Damn, what I mean is, well, I'm wondering if you liked to do this again? I need a plus one for a couple of upcoming events and I'd rather go with you instead of someone who'd get the wrong idea. I want to focus on my last season, not my dating life, you know?"

My heart fell. For a split second, I did think he was hitting on me. *See what happens when you get your hopes up over a guy like him?* I held myself together the best I could.

"You're asking me to be what, a fake girlfriend? I thought you'd shot down that idea." There was no way I'd let him know just how disappointed I was. Because I shouldn't be. We'd just met a week ago for like all of five minutes.

Brock waved his hands. "No, sorry. I guess I should have realized that Kelsey told you about that, and yes, at first, I was against it. But now I'm reconsidering. We're getting along pretty well, and we even like a lot of the same things. But don't worry, I'm not asking you to move in with me or anything. I have another event next week and the winter extravaganza in LA in January and maybe attend some home games in April? And there may be, uh, a few more events, but my agent hasn't verified them yet."

He thought things were going well between us? He must have a really low bar for measuring dates. I mean, there may have been a couple moments of really good conversation, but I hadn't thought I'd was being especially alluring or engaging. I was just being me. Then there was his upbeat attitude that was slowly making its way under my radar *"What if Brock actually likes you, Thea?"* Could I let myself hope that he might?

He kept talking, but all I could think was I'd be up close and personal to all his hard angles and muscles. Would I be able to keep my hands to myself?

"So, as soon as I know, I'd let you know. What do you think? Could you help me out? I'd be glad to return the favor if you have anything you need to attend. I know how tough it is to show up alone to places where everyone else is coupled up."

"How about you think about it? Give it a day or two." The look on his handsome face was so hopeful I found myself returning his grin and thinking about it.

The waiter saved me from saying anything as he offered the bill to Brock. "Oh, wait. I'm paying, remember?" I tried to grab the small tray, but he pulled it out of my reach.

"No, this wasn't 'the' date. I mean, this was a nice dinner, but it doesn't live up to the advertised 'fantasy date' with a bachelor. I want you to get your money's worth." He winked and flashed his sexy smile. I bit my lip to keep from laughing, then squeezed my thighs as his gaze turned hot, challenging. Dammit, not only was he handsome, but he was funny too.

"I'll save that for after you agree and go to the Hospice Winter Ball with me next week."

"Wow, confident, aren't you?" There was a snap to my words I wasn't proud of. I frowned then looked away. Yet another item to add to the growing list of unexpected turn-ons only Brock could ignite because, if any other man said such things, I would shut them down immediately.

He didn't answer right away. Instead, he did that stupid sexy thing with his mouth again, holding my gaze. Holding it so long that as nonchalantly as I could, I finished off my ice water to cool my body's low simmer as it threatened to go full boil. Who knew a man could affect me so intimately with just a look?

"Why the frown? Is this the grumpy side Kelsey warned me about?" Brock chuckled.

Oh, no she didn't. How could she?

I lifted my lips then used my calm voice. "I'm not grumpy. Guarded? Yes. Wary? Most of the time. And suspicious of your charm? Definitely. But I'm not grumpy. And I wish everyone would stop saying 'I'm the grumpy one.'" Crossing my arms, I willed him to change the subject.

Instead, Brock's mouth lifted back into another sexy smile. "Well, Thea. I guess you'll just have to prove everyone wrong and take me up on my offer, won't you?" Brock said softly. He took out his wallet and settled the bill, breaking the spell.

Oh yeah, I was in so much trouble.

CHAPTER SIX

BROCK

Two days later and I still hadn't heard anything from Thea. I began to question whether I should have rushed her, but something deep down told me if I hadn't, then I wouldn't have another opportunity.

There was something about her standoffish behavior that drew me in. Maybe what was written about opposites attracting was true because I wanted to learn as much as I could about Thea Lynch, even if it meant getting her to pretend to be my girlfriend.

The press was having a field day with the photo of us having dinner the other night. But, one of the Kardashian's had another break up and thank the media gods, it had dialed down the fervor over my dating life.

I'd already worked out for the day, but I was still keyed up and needed another outlet. Keeping fit in the off season had become a priority the older I got, but that's not what had me chasing endorphins. It was because of Thea.

I debated calling her if only to hear her voice again. On the drive home the other night I'd made sure to keep a safe distance between us knowing that if our shoulders had barely brushed, I'd be on her like a rookie sliding into first base after placing a perfect bunt down the third base line.

Dammit. I adjusted my dick again and headed for the shower. Just thinking about her had me hard. I stripped out of my workout clothes on my way to my shower and reached the door handle just as my cell chimed. I debated for half a second. Not many people had my number. And it could be Thea.

I did an about face and swiped it off my night table, knowing that if I didn't check, I'd be wondering during my shower who had texted me. But it wasn't a text. It was a voicemail notification. And it was from her number. I thumbed through the screens until her soft, sexy voice filled my bedroom.

"Um, Hi. This is Thea. Lynch."

I grinned. Like I wouldn't know who she is.

"Could you give me a call when you get this message? Bye."

The shower could wait. I hit call back and waited. She picked up on the second ring.

"Thea Lynch."

"Hey, gorgeous."

Her heavy breathing came through loud and clear and I held back a moan. It was like I was

seventeen again instead of thirty-seven, and my dick perked up to prove it.

"Oh, that was fast. Um, thanks for getting back to me so quickly." Thea's voice sounded breathy, with a hint of excitement. Damn, I hoped so.

"Of course. Although there are plenty of things I take

my time over, but calling you back isn't one of them." Cheesy? Sure, but I wanted her a bit off balance. I planned on doing plenty of flirting, complementing and saying things to make her laugh. Anything it took to make sure she'd agree to my request.

"Oh, yeah, that's nice. So, I've given your proposal some thought and..."

Damn, she's killing me. Why was she pausing? I jumped in as if she agreed. "That's great. For once I'm looking forward to attending one of these things. Seeing you again will definitely make it more enjoyable." Too much. Maybe, but I didn't care. Whatever it took.

"Okay, first, you don't have to flatter me. I've decided to help you out. And second, as long as we don't go overboard with social media or PDA, I'll be your pretend girlfriend. But only for three months."

Thea's serious tone returned. But when she'd mentioned PDA, a lightbulb went off. Yeah, I wasn't going to promise anything of the sort. "That's great. Thank you. I'd, uh, already mentioned something to my agent about it. I hope you don't mind. He does have a few ideas for some other photos we could post online."

Silence. All I could hear was office background noise. "Thea, you still with me?"

She cleared her throat and my dick twitched. I looked up at my ceiling and shook my head. Yeah, I guess my dry spell had lasted a little too long.

"I'm here. That uh, sounds fine. It hasn't been too crazy since our dinner at the resort was posted. But, maybe not let anyone else know, though. The fewer people who know the truth, the better. You, me, your agent, and Kelsey. Oh, and Harlowe. She's one of my closest friends and she also works here. But she's sworn to secrecy. In fact, her husband Zak.

Zak Carter, you might know him. His company runs player security for the Outlaws?"

Yeah, I knew Zak. He's a good guy and would keep our secret. "Sure, I know him. I heard he got married last year. Is Harlowe going to tell him?"

"Not unless she has to. But she also had a couple of ideas for us. I've got a meeting to go to, but I wanted to let you know so that if you still wanted me to go to the winter ball with you this weekend—"

"Yes!" I grimaced at the volume of my response. Shit, I didn't want her to think I was desperate. Well, desperate for her anyway.

"Okay, great."

"Great. I'll text you the details, but it begins at seven on Saturday, so how about I pick you up, say six thirty?"

"Sure. I'll be ready."

"Great." *Dude, you need to work on your conversation skills.*

"See you then. Bye."

I sat staring at my cell. Thoughts of seeing her again and getting the chance to put my hands on her, holding her while we danced or stood close while we chatted with people, showing off our new relationship and hopefully getting a chance to kiss her, had me looking down.

Still naked and very, very hard. Grinning, I made my way to the shower where thoughts of Thea in my arms, under me, pounding into her had me shouting out her name as I took myself in hand and imagining all the ways I wanted to make her scream mine.

CHAPTER SEVEN

THEA

The days following our date and my agreement to be Brock's "girlfriend" flew by. Things were slow at work with the season over, but they'd be ramping back up in December. The players may get a few months off, but the front office ran pretty much all year.

I stood in front of my closet and debated. Sexy or not sexy? Did I want Brock drooling or yawning and question his decision based on the formal dress I wore tonight? According to Harlowe and my sister, who I caved and told the truth, I should definitely go sexy. This was Brock Cameron, after all. The Pineville Playboy, at least that's what the media would lead you to believe, but I was having my doubts.

He could have chosen anyone to go along with this idea, but he'd asked me. That meant he at least thought I was pretty, right? Ugh, I hated how I was almost thirty-five years old, and I still wanted the cute boy to like me.

An hour later, the ring of my doorbell had me sucking in a breath and counting to ten. I blew it out slowly, picked up my clutch, and answered the door.

My jaw dropped at the sight awaiting me. If I'd thought he was handsome in his tux at the auction, I was so wrong. Nothing compared to the dangerously seductive Brock standing on my porch. It was more than the tailored designer suit; it was the man. His eyes flashed and his nostrils flared as his gaze roamed my body. "You look..." His eyes locked on my face, and he let out an audible breath. The corner of his mouth curled up. "Thea you are stunning." He handed me a single, perfect red rose. "I'm going to have to keep you close so no other guy thinks he can make a move on you."

Unaccustomed to such compliments, I snapped from the fairy tale haze I allowed myself to fall into. "Thank you. Let me go put these in water and I'll be right back."

He waited on the porch while I teetered on my heels into my kitchen and scrambled to find something to put the rose in. I allowed myself a quick inhale of the flower's spicy scent. When was the last time a man had given me flowers, not once, but now twice? Never. I couldn't let it sway me into thinking it was anything but window dressing. He was playing a part. That's all.

I shouldn't read anything into it. He was simply being nice.

But the look he wore as I approached my front door was anything but nice. The power of his interested stare had my nipples going hard. I'd chosen the fitted dress since it flattered my curvy form. Tonight might not be real, but the look he was giving me sure felt it. And feeling pretty would give me the boost I needed to be on Brock's arm all evening.

I locked up and took his offered hand as he led me to his

car. I'm not sure what I thought he would drive, but it wasn't the Ford Raptor parked in my driveway. When he opened the passenger door, a step lowered from the side of the truck. I looked at him and he flushed. It was cute.

"It's not a limo, but I wanted to drive my own rig."

"Nice rig, Cameron." I grinned at him and took his hand as he helped me up into the high-end vehicle. I took in the new car smell and marveled at the console, rubbing my hand along the supple leather.

"Boys and their toys, huh?"

Brock's face brightened at my words. "It's been a long time since I played with toys, Thea. But for you, I'm up for anything." He started the truck and reversed out of my driveway.

His flirty response had my mouth drying up.

My belly flipped, and I held back a moan.

Then I wiggled in my seat and clenched my thighs together. Again, the immediate effect he had on me had me reeling. Every time. Three times now. Not sure I could handle any more of Brock's lethal brand of flirting, I doubled my resolve and called on my inner ice queen. I couldn't afford to fall for him when all of this wasn't real.

I cleared my throat and folded my hands in my lap. "When we're alone, you don't need to flirt with me. So, let's save it for an audience, okay?"

"You think that was me flirting with you?"

"Wasn't it?" The sharpness of his words threw me off guard.

"I guess if you have to ask, then I'm not doing it right. But one thing you can count on from me is honesty. If I feel it, then I'm going to say it and that is as real as it gets for me. So believe me when I flirt with you or compliment you, that's real. Because it was my choice to ask you to help me out. I guess I could get through this media frenzy another way, but I took a chance. I wanted to spend more time with you and that is real. I'm sorry that I confused the issue with this whole fake girlfriend thing. That's on me. If I'm way off, let me know. But I don't think I am."

It took a lot to leave me speechless, but he'd managed it. Could I believe him? Did he want me?

"Convince me, Thea. Make me believe our connection isn't real."

The valet opened my door and saved me from answering. I shifted from the dare in Brock's steely eyed gaze, pasted a smile on my face, stepped down, and waited for him to guide us onto the red carpet. Instead of paying attention to the shouted requests for a picture from the media lined along the sidewalk, his heated look as he pulled me close sent shivers through me. "Your silence is only encouraging me, Thea. I plan on flirting with you the rest of the evening. I hope you're ready."

Me too.

I wanted this to be real, and it was the scariest thing I've ever felt.

CHAPTER EIGHT

BROCK

The night was a living hell, and I wasn't referring to the reason for attending. I was happy to give my time for the charity. What had me seething was the attention Thea was receiving from other men, even when I was glued to her side. And she didn't seem to notice.

Every smile she returned, and every conversation she engaged in, made me greedy for her attention. I wanted to be on the receiving end of her smiles, and the easy way she interacted with everyone but me. Whenever I touched her elbow or placed my hand on the small of her back, I felt her body stiffen, then she'd shift slightly away from me. She was driving me crazy and had me half hard all evening.

I had to remind myself Thea was a professional. She worked in PR and was used to interacting with people where all I wanted to do was leave and talk her into inviting me in so I could peel her sexy gown down her perfect curves. No longer was this night about pretending to be a couple. I wanted, needed, to get her underneath me and show her just how real I wanted our fake relationship to be.

When the time finally came to leave, I rushed her out the door and into my truck. As if we had an unspoken agreement, the drive to her place was silent. Loaded silence. The air in the cab was filled with electricity and the anticipation of what might happen between us had me shifting and adjusting myself.

"Do you believe in fate, Thea?" Staring straight ahead at her house through the windshield, I used my peripheral vision to note her response.

She snorted. It was full of denial, but her hand shook as she swept back her hair. I grinned and kept talking.

"So, you're going to deny that when we collided in the hallway that you didn't feel anything. Or when we had dinner last week, or tonight when we danced? Tell me you felt nothing. I'll walk you to the door, and we can end this fake relationship and move on."

Her body jolted at my suggestion. Ah, not as unaffected as she wanted me to think.

"This doesn't make sense. We just met. I mean, I'm not your usual type. How about I just save us both anymore time and heart--. Anyway, I'm really sorry I've wasted yours, Brock. I should have known better."

"Sometimes things don't make sense. They just are. And opening yourself to happiness and connection...otherwise what's the point? And you are so my type, you have no idea." We talk over the other and I see the moment she realizes what I said.

I see her shake her head, but it only spurs me to keep going. First, I need to touch her, even it's for the last time. I get out, walk around the front of my truck, and open her door. Taking her hand, I help her down and walk her to her front door. Now or never. She makes me nervous, but in a good way. In a way that I know she's the one. Mav would be so proud.

Turning her to face me, I take her hands in mine. "So, you don't believe my attraction to you is real, right? I bet you think I'm only being nice. Well, I am nice. And sure, I prefer to look on the positive side most of the time. And maybe the guys call me Mr. Sunshine in the locker room, but I can play dirty with the best of them. Do you want to get dirty with me, Thea?"

Loose tendrils had escaped her hair clip and were framing her face and I brush them aside and cup her face. How could a woman as beautiful as her think she wasn't my type or that I couldn't be attracted to her? Lost in the fire emanating from her eyes, I watch as she fights her reaction to me. Her chin juts out and lifts and I want to kiss the obstinance right out of her.

I pinned my gaze on her, daring her to look away from me. "That the best you got? Well, let me share a secret, Thea. Whatever inner voice is telling you that you're not pretty enough or glamorous enough is lying. Don't shake your head, sweetheart. It's true."

Cursing the sudden urge to strangle whatever man made her believe any of those things made my blood boil. Damn the fool that made her feel as if she had to put up some kind of wall to protect herself. Against me.

Women had to put up with such bullshit when it came to beauty standards. I never did get why being stick thin had become so coveted. Most men I knew wanted a woman with soft curves.

"Still don't believe me? Well then, how about you explain why I'm standing here rock hard? For you."

Confusion and a bit of sadness appeared in her watery

eyes, and I wanted to wipe both immediately away. "Oh, sweetheart, if you let me in, I'm going to enjoy showing you just how much I want you."

Her mouth opened into a perfect "O" at my words.

My cock pulsed, my heart raced, and hope filled me that I'd broken through the shield she'd put up moments after we'd collided.

"I'm so close to kissing you right now. Let me know now if you want me to leave otherwise, I'm—"

Her mouth pressed on mine and, lord, she had the sweetest lips I'd ever tasted. I pulled her in, cupped the back of her head, and devoured her sweet little moans.

I'd prepared myself for her to push me away. When she didn't, I pushed her up against her front door, placed a leg between her thighs and ground my aching cock against her softness. She let out a soft gasp, mouthing "yes" against my ear. She captured the lobe between her teeth and bit hard enough to send a rush of blood straight to my cock. "Sweetheart, you're playing with fire. We need to get inside."

Thea laughed. The sexy sound went straight to my cock, making me harder than I'd been in a very long time. She lifted her handbag, took out her key, and slipped it into the lock on the first try. I urged her inside, slammed and locked the door. "Bedroom?"

"The couch is closer." Her silky voice wrapped around my cock and led me to the oversized sectional. Thank fuck, because I was a goner. I needed to be inside her now.

She shimmed out of her dress, stepped out of her heels and reached for my jacket. I whipped it off, tugged at my tie, and kicked off my shoes. Her hands fumbled over the buttons of my shirt. "Screw it." I tore it off my body and picked her up. I placed my hands under her curvy ass and carried her the short distance to the couch and let her go.

Her shriek was music to my ears. "Tell me you're sure, Thea." I held her gaze as I pulled my wallet from my slacks and withdrew two condoms and tossed them on the coffee table. Her eyes widened at the movement.

"Two?"

"What can I say? I'm nothing if not optimistic. And I'm pretty sure our first time is going to go way too fast. So plan on a second round where I can take my time, savoring every inch." She blushed and bit her bottom lip. "Promises, promises."

"Oh, I'm here for it. Lay back for me and spread those legs for me." She sucked in a breath at my demand, but didn't hesitate. She leaned back on her elbows and opened herself to me. Without taking my gaze from her glistening mound, I unbuckled my slacks and in one movement took them and my underwear off. I palmed my cock and smiled at her indrawn breath. "You make that sound a lot. I hope that's a good thing?" I kneeled on the floor in front of her, placing my hands over her thighs, nudging them wide.

"Oh, my." Her head fell back, exposing her long neck, raising her still covered breasts, and I had to slow down or I was going to lose it.

"No, mine. All mine. Take your bra off. That's it, nice and slow." I cupped a breast and flicked its hard nipple. She squirmed at the contact while I thumbed her clit at the same time. "So wet. Lord, you're fucking gorgeous. You know that, right?" She started to shake her head, and I stopped her, grasping her chin as gently as I could. "Look at me. See how hard I am for you? I want to do so many things to you right now. I can't make up my mind where to begin. Do you get that? It's more than physical attraction or sex. I want to make you feel so good you'll never doubt me again."

My thumb hovered over her opening, touching but not

moving. I felt her body's response to my words as her creaminess spilled onto my flesh. "Oh sweetheart, I'm going to make you cum so hard, scream my name until your throat is raw and until I'm speechless and spent inside of you."

She nodded, excitement shining brightly from her dark brown eyes, gone darker by her desire. I dipped between her thighs and licked along her slick folds. Her hips lifted toward me. She sighed my name, but I wanted more. Flicking my tongue against her clit, I suckled and ran the tip over and over the spot that brought her to the edge. I felt her fingers thread through my hair, urging me. I slowed my pace, then softly blew on her swollen flesh. "Tell me what you want?"

Lifting herself closer to me, Thea sighed. "You know what I want. Please." Dragging out the plea, I chuckled and started over again. This time I spread her folds and dived deep with my tongue, pleasuring her until she shouted my name. I eased back and gave all my attention to her sweet spot, rubbing her till she came. Triumph rode me as she rolled her hips, her inner walls clamping down when I added a finger into her slick channel.

"Brock." She whispered my name. "That was...." I looked at her face. Soft and relaxed, she wore a beautiful smile.

"Damn, you knock me off balance, you know that?" Grabbing a condom, I rolled it on and leaned over her. Trailing kisses along her stomach, between her breasts and paying extra attention to each globe. I finally took her lips, kissing her breathlessly. Her legs wrapped around my hips, pulling me in.

"I need you."

"Oh, sweetheart. You have me. Guide me in."

Her hot hand circled the base of my cock and with our

gazes locked, she brought me to her entrance. What I saw in her gaze made my heart skip a beat before I slid inside her warmth, building a steady rhythm that had her begging me to move faster. Pounding into her, we came together, and I swear I heard a whisper in my head that said, "you're home."

CHAPTER NINE

THEA

The morning after the winter ball, I woke up to Brock placing kisses along the small of my back. His stamina was impressive and had me changing my opinion of athletes. Must be all that exercising and playing baseball. He was a selfless lover, so much so that not having a third condom didn't faze him. Instead, he made sure I enjoyed his amazingly talented tongue. Just thinking about it ignited a full body flush.

Sundays were spent catching up on household chores and the occasional nap, and today was one of those days. I woke up a bit groggy around four, shuffled into the kitchen to look for something to eat. Taking a plate into the front room, I settled into my couch, and spent the next half hour eating and daydreaming.

Brenley's text tone broke me out of my fantasy of Brock and me being a real couple and little girls with his hazel eyes and dark hair. I knew such thoughts were dangerous, considering all the times I told my friends I didn't believe in love.

Have you checked out insta today?

I snorted. **I've been busy. What's up?**

You. Brock. Tons of pix of the two of you dancing. And well, just look, then call me. ASAP.

Sighing, I grabbed my cell and pulled up the app. There were a lot of photos of us, but nothing I wouldn't have posted myself. As I thumbed through the feed, a couple more close ups of us appeared. My jaw dropped.

I quickly called Brenley and walked to my office and opened my laptop, bringing up Insta on the browser.

"What is going on between you and Brock?" Brenley's voice rose on each word. "Are you holding out on me, because you two look in—"

"No. Nothing. I'm helping him out. I told you, it's temporary." My sister snort laughed. Yeah, we had that in common.

"Whatever. You're not that good of an actor. Spill it, sis. Do you have feelings for Brock Cameron?" Oh, she knew better than to go there with me. We didn't talk about our upbringing much. Why should we? We knew how screwed up it was. No need to rehash it. Our mom was gone, and our father, well, he might as well be gone. No, there was no way what I saw was in those photos would change my mind.

"Thea, calm down. You sound like you're having an asthma attack, sweetie. It's okay. This is good. I'm happy for you. And Brock Cameron, all I can say is *wowza*. He's a hottie, and you deserve him."

No, no, this wasn't happening. "Brenley, stop it." I begged.

"Well, just look at those pictures again. At the way he's looking at you and how you're looking at him. When you're ready to talk, when you need to talk. Call me. I'm going to the shop. I'm having a ranunculus emergency."

It was my turn to snort-laugh. "That sounds made up."

"I wish it was. Love you."

"Love you."

Brenley was wrong about what she thought she saw in those photos. Of course, Brock and I spent most of the night next to each other. That was the whole point. We talked about a lot of things. It was kind of hard not to learn more about one another. And the things I learned, and how he treated me, had been a big reason why we'd ended the night in bed.

He'd made me feel special and looking back on the evening, I didn't once feel like we were faking anything. In fact, we seemed to fit like two lost puzzle pieces, speaking with so many people that soon we were being complimented on seeming like an old married couple. That had thrown me by the second time I'd heard it. It had come from Maverick, and Kelsey had given him the side eye and dragged him away.

I stared hard at the pictures again. I'd never seen pictures of me looking so happy, relaxed and...no, that... wasn't even possible. I'd just met him. These pictures were taken before we had toe curling sex. There was no way what I was reading on my face was anything but a woman having a good time. I slammed shut my laptop.

I was *not* in love with Brock Cameron. It wasn't possible.

CHAPTER TEN

BROCK

The days flew by as Thea and I found time to be together between her schedule and my workouts. We were becoming close, but I felt she was holding something back from me. Something important.

I'd catch her looking at me with an odd look on her face and when I asked her what was wrong, she'd smile and say nothing.

It wasn't nothing. But I didn't push. In fact, we fell into a routine of sorts. We went out to dinner every other night this past week and then would end up at my house or hers. We'd dropped off TMZ's radar. Seems we weren't the exciting "it" couple they were looking for.

Two weeks in, I was sure about my feelings for Thea. In fact, it had become so important to me I was more concerned about making her mine than I was winning another championship. I had to figure out a way to tell her

I'd fallen in love with her from the first moment we met without her laughing in my face.

Tonight, I was meeting up with my cousins who'd flown in for the holidays at O'Malley's.

"Cameron! Over here." Dax waved me over to a table they'd snagged in the packed bar. I paused to sign a couple autographs and pose for a few pictures.

"Hey, Brock. Where's your girlfriend?" One of the pub's regulars shouted. "You need to bring her with you next time. She'll class up the place." Grinning, I nodded and said, "You're not wrong."

Moving quickly to avoid any more interactions with fans, I reached the table and gratefully grabbed the pint of beer Dax had waiting for me. They both knew what I was up against whenever in public, especially in Pineville.

Dax was a NASCAR driver, and Easton, younger by just a year, was in his eighth year with the NFL. The media had a field day whenever the three of us were together.

Easton typically wouldn't have been able to attend, but unfortunately he'd suffered an Achilles heel injury keeping him out for the rest of the year. He'd make a full recovery, but the process was slow. Even with his left foot and lower leg in a boot, women still flocked to him. Hopefully, tonight we wouldn't have to deal with too many fans or photographers looking for their exclusive shot.

Sitting down, my cousins raised their mugs, and we saluted each other. Taking a deep pull of the house draft, I sighed. "Damn that's good."

Slade Johansson, the pub's head bartender, delivered a new pitcher and a plate of my favorite, Angus sliders, and a basket of fries. They'd recently hired a new chef, Taya, and business had increased since she'd arrived with her new twist on pub food.

"Hey, Brock. I didn't know these two were related to you. That's some gene pool your family has. Any more pro athletes I should know about?" Slade hooked his thumb at my cousins and Easton laughed. "By the way, I've got the rest of the staff on notice to help keep overeager fans away from your table. Anything else you guys need, just wave. I'll be taking care of you tonight." He flashed us a wide grin and headed back to the bar.

For a moment, all the female eyes that had been on our table followed Slade as he walked away. The bartender looked like he could be a pro athlete and attracted his fair share of female attention. Hopefully, that'd help us out, and we'd be left alone. I was looking forward to catching up before the rest of our extended family arrived. It would be controlled chaos at my parents' house. How my mom and aunts put it all together year after year still amazed me.

"So glad you guys could both make it." I grabbed a slider and polished it off in two bites. I reached for another and sighed. Man, Taya knew her way to a man's heart or at least stomach. Plus, she was just my type, curvy and fun to be around. But she had a couple of college-age kids and wasn't looking for more, so I never pursued her.

One thing I definitely wanted was children. Did Thea want kids? I hoped so. It was so easy to imagine her pregnant with my child.

Sensing Dax and Easton were staring at me, "What? Do I have something on my face?" Grabbing a napkin, I paused to find them with expectant looks on their faces.

"Nope. We're just over here waiting for you to stuff your face, then tell us about this chick who bought you at that auction gig." Easton finished his slider in one bite, looking like an overgrown squirrel with his cheeks puffed out instead of a 6' 2" wide receiver grinning as he chewed his food.

Throwing my wadded-up napkin at him, I said, "It's a good thing you got grandad's good looks, otherwise no woman would put up with you chewing with your mouth open."

"What? It's a great slider. I think I'm in love. I need to meet the chef. Didn't Slade say her name was Taya? Maybe he'll introduce me." Easton rubbed his hands together, then poked his brother. "Your turn."

Looking from one cousin to the other, I shook my head. "First, she's way out of your league. And second, what do you want to know about Thea? I'm sure you've seen the posts online. We're... dating."

"And?" Dax prompted.

Usually, we never discussed women. Well, that's not entirely true, but the days of sharing our conquests had long passed.

"And what?"

Easton polished off another slider and leaned forward. "We're here for you, bro. If you want to talk about, you know relationship stuff."

"What is up with you two? You starting a blog or what?" Then it hit me. "Hey, your mom didn't put you guys up to all these questions, did she? Or more specifically, did my mom ask your mom to get you two to shake me down for info on Thea?"

Dax laughed.

Easton grimaced.

Bingo. I guess I shouldn't be surprised. My parents had dropped hints over the years about my single life, worried that I was missing out on having a wife and kids. But I wasn't going to get married just because it was expected, or because I was getting older. It would be for love and nothing less.

"You gotta admit, Brock, you haven't even come close to a long-term relationship. Are you sure about her? I mean, you've never even been engaged. I always thought you'd be the Playboy Player for the rest of your life."

Sometimes the truth hurt and sometimes it's just what a man needed.

"Dax, coming from you, that's a low blow. Maybe we should talk about your long list of ex-girlfriends. But I'm going to let it go. And remind you and Easton, when I'm off the market, both of you are gonna be up front and center on not just our family's radar, but the media's. I'll be sure and drop your names in the ear of a certain photographer I know. You two, more than anyone, know how much crap I put up with from people that don't really know me."

Easton held up his hands, then pointed to his brother. "Hey, keep me out of this. Anything you want to know about Dax's love life hit me up. Ow!" Dax turned to his brother, "Dude, kick me again and it'll be the last time you use that leg."

Shit, this was not how I wanted tonight to go. I hardly ever got to hang out with them, and they knew better than anyone else in our family the same pressures a professional athlete was under by having our personal lives scrutinized by the public and the press. "Alright, you two. This isn't high school. Finish your beer and—"

"Wait. Easton, I think I know what's happening here. Brock, our easygoing cousin, has finally been bitten. I think he and Thea are doing more than just 'dating'."

I mean, he wasn't wrong. And I did want to run it by them. They were the closest thing I had to brothers.

"Okay, okay. What do you want to know?" I put my

arms on the table, folding one over the other, and leaned forward. "Thea knocked me on my ass from the moment I met her. She's all I can think about, and what began as a way to help me out has turned into something more real than I've ever had before."

I lowered my voice. "Yup. She's the one. But I need to up my game. She's so, so guarded. Her friends tease her about being too much of a grump, but I've seen her when she lets her guard down, and man, I like her." I signaled Slade.

"Oh, shit." Dax and Easton said in unison.

"Are you telling us you're in love with this chick?" Easton asked.

"Her name is Thea, and yeah." A part of me felt guilty for telling my cousins first.

"Have either one of you told a woman you love her?"

Both men shook their heads.

"Nah, I have time. It's you and Dax who need to carry on the family name. I'm gonna coast till forty at least."

"You're such a dufus, East," Dax turned away from his brother, then looked at me, "And if she's really the one, you need to go big."

Easton ignored Dax's insult. "Yeah, one of those grand gestures. Surprise her somehow."

Slade dropped off the bill. Deep in thought, I missed the opportunity to grab it first.

"Brock, you still with us?"

Grinning, I finished my beer and stood. "What do you guys think about a surprise birthday party? Thea's thirty-fifth is next week, the day after Christmas. You still going to be around?"

Suddenly, not only telling Thea how I felt about her, but showing her became my number one priority.

CHAPTER ELEVEN

THEA

A BOUQUET OF FLOWERS ARRIVED THIRTY MINUTES before Brock was supposed to show up for dinner at my place. I inhaled their scent and arranged them in my favorite cut-glass vase, placing them on the center of my dining table. He'd used my sister's floral shop, which was super sweet that he was giving his business to her.

Setting the sauce to simmer, I checked the chicken and adjusted the timer. He was due any minute and my hands shook as I took off my apron. Tonight, I wanted to tell him all the things I hadn't shared. Well, the important ones anyway. I wanted him to understand why I had to stop seeing him. It was getting too hard being around him, loving him when he was just playing a part.

I'm sure he'd understand when I explained my side of things. It had been fun. The sex was amazing, but it was time to put an end to our fake dating.

Looking around the kitchen and the dining room to

assure I had everything in place, I took the chilled chardonnay from the fridge and uncorked it. The chime of the front doorbell rang out. I set the wine bottle in the ice bucket and went to answer the door.

"Hi."

"Hi, gorgeous." Brock gathered me in his arms, kicked the door shut, and kissed me senseless.

How could he affect me like this? Every. Single. Time. I had to hold firm, otherwise I'd forget all the reasons I told myself why I had to end things.

Pushing against his chest, I broke our kiss. "C'mon. Dinner's ready. Your timing is perfect."

"You know what else would be perfect? You. In bed." He grabbed my waist and began to walk me backward to my room. I grabbed onto his biceps and let out a low moan. I allowed myself a few moments to run my hands over the steel ridges of his muscles. I'd never felt more desired than when I was in his arms.

"Brock, as much as I want that too, let's have dinner first, please?"

He must have picked up on the urgency in my voice and set me back down. "Of course. Are you okay, you sound...off."

I pulled out of his arms and led him to the table. "Could you pour the wine?"

He nodded and filled the glasses. I took the chicken from the oven, grabbed the potato and veggie casserole, and sat down.

I couldn't quite look him in the eye, so I took a fortifying sip of my wine, then began serving the food. "Even though we've been spending a lot of time together lately, well things have gotten complicated."

"I like how complicated things have gotten. And I know

you like it when I touch you right—"

"Brock, stop. I'm trying to have a serious conversation." Brock waggled his eyebrows at me. I had to bite my lip to keep from laughing.

"What we're doing, it's just...becoming too much for me. And I feel like we need to talk before we go any further." Peeking up at him, his expression still unreadable.

Ignoring my food, I pushed forward. "I want to begin with I'm not upset, mad or anything like that, so don't worry. But I've come to a decision. That we, well me, I can't continue to be your fake girlfriend." I paused and looked directly at him. He deserved that. I didn't want to hurt him.

"There are things that I've begun to feel. About me and my past and...I think it's not fair to you or to me."

I really wanted him to say something, anything, but the look on his face hadn't changed. Maybe for him it was all about the great sex, but I knew I wanted more and I couldn't ask for more without at least giving him an opportunity to walk away.

"Um, okay. So you may have noticed I don't have a sparkling, positive personality? Yeah, well, of course you have. Anyway, one of the reasons I'm like this, why I tend to be...well, serious is that my parents were pretty screwed up, emotionally, that is. Their marriage was awful. My father, he was a cold SOB, but my mother stuck it out with him. All she wanted was to be loved and to be shown physical affection, not just sex, you know. So, anyway, she stayed. My siblings and I ignored the situation as teenagers did. At the time, not realizing how truly messed up our family was. Our mom died from cancer about five years ago. And I swore I'd never be like her. That I wouldn't give my heart, my body to a man who didn't or couldn't..." My voice caught in my throat and I took a couple deep breaths.

His features had softened the more I spoke, but he still hadn't said anything. "For the longest time, I thought all men were like that. Then when I was in college, I began to think maybe they weren't. Hoping they weren't because I had the biggest crush on this guy from the swim team. One night at a party, I gathered the courage to talk to him. He blew me off and said some hurtful things about my weight. Then he made a big production out of it, in front of my friends. He was drunk, but it hurt. So, the walls went up, and I didn't let any man get close to me. Until you."

I blew out a long breath and took a big gulp of wine. My gaze went to Brock's hands, which had been resting on the table on either side of his place setting during my speech. His knuckles had gone white.

"I know this is crazy to dump on you like this, but I wanted you to know what made me the way I am. And to thank you."

"To thank me? For fake dating you?" Brock shifted in his seat.

I panicked and did the opposite of what I'd planned. "I love you!"

Shock filled his handsome face. And before I could take it back or explain what I really wanted to tell him, he was at my side, pulling me into his arms and lovingly cupped my face in his large hands.

"You love me?"

Nodding my head, I began to cry. "I do."

"Oh, sweet, Thea. Don't cry. I love you too."

Staring at him, my eyes went wide, and I started to cry harder. Brock rubbed my back in slow, comforting circles until I calmed down. I let out two small hiccups, buried my face into his chest, then let out a long sigh. "They're happy tears." I mumbled into his chest. "Oh, gawd. I'm such a mess. I didn't plan on telling you I love you. I was going to end things, but I guess I freaked and I couldn't imagine my life without you. Oh, I never thought this would happen."

"What's that?"

Wiping my eyes, I tipped my head back. "You. Us. Love. It's so fast and I just—" another hiccup rocked me, and I shut my eyes and groaned.

Feeling Brock's chest rumble and shake below my hands, I sighed. "Ugh, not the reaction I was going for."

"Oh, babe. This is you, honest and raw, sharing your heart with me. I will treasure this memory, hiccups and all." He placed a soft kiss on my lips, then brushed away my remaining tears.

"I'm going to tell you a secret. I was a goner at the auction. In the hallway when you plowed into me. And seeing your shocked expression, the look you gave me before you slammed that wall down, I was sure you felt the same. And sometimes that's how it happens. Instant connection, love at first sight. Because it was for me. And it has only grown the more time we've spent together."

I didn't argue. How could I considering the way my heart fluttered? Then my stomach flipped and my whole body shivered at hearing him tell me those three little words. He was nothing like my father, and I was definitely not my mother. And suddenly I had to tell him my own secret.

"After I won the bid for you, I couldn't go up on that stage. I was afraid everyone, especially you, would see how attracted I was to you. And I never let my guard down in public. I called myself crazy as I beelined out of that ballroom."

"But?"

"Why do you think there's a but? It was crazy. Crazy

smart." Standing on tiptoe, I kissed his smiling lips, tugged his shirt up and ran my hands along his firm stomach, then reached for his belt. "The dinner's cold. Take me to bed."

"The couch is closer." He scooped me up and carried me into the living room.

Who was I to argue?

EPILOGUE

One week later

BROCK

Slade rang the bell behind the bar at O'Malley's and called out to our gathered friends and family, bringing their attention to where I stood next to Thea. "Thank you all for attending. I'd like to take just a few minutes from the fun to wish my girl a very happy birthday. She doesn't like the spotlight, as I've well learned, but I'd like to take this moment and celebrate her on this special day."

I pulled her to my side and grinned down at her with my heart thundering in my ears. I loved making her blush. She was so damn beautiful and having her in my life permanently had become more than necessary. I didn't want another day to go by that she didn't know how much she meant to me.

Clearing my throat, I kept my gaze locked on Thea, and spoke loud enough for everyone in the room to hear.

"Thea, before I give you your gift, I wanted to begin by saying that sometimes you don't get what you want or ask for. But, sometimes, you receive exactly what you need—who you need—and at just the right time. And for me, that's you and it's now. I knew immediately you were more than a want for me." Wolf whistles rang out, and her cheek's flushed darker pink.

I dropped a kiss on her lips, then spoke directly to everyone in the room to settle my nerves.

"A few of you knew this, but most didn't. On our first date, I asked Thea to be my fake girlfriend to get the media off my back during my last season. Thankfully, she took pity on me and agreed. What she didn't know was that I was determined to make her my girlfriend for real. And it was a great relief that our very cautious, sometimes guarded, but not grumpy, Thea, agreed." I paused as laughter rang out through the pub. Even Thea's.

"But I've decided being my girlfriend isn't enough. That I can't wait to begin living the rest of our lives together." Pulling the ring from my pocket, I knelt down and took her left hand in mine. I felt her body begin to shake and saw tears form as she briefly looked at the diamond solitaire before gazing at me in surprise. For a split second, I wished we were alone so I could kiss and touch her the way I wanted without embarrassing her.

The gathered crowd's laughter was replaced with a few shocked gasps and shouts of "alright" plus at least one exclamation of: "About damn time!" I wasn't sure, but I think it came from Maverick.

"I love you so much, Thea. Will you be my wife?"

The woman who stole my heart and opened hers to me

dazzled me with her smile. Happiness radiated from her. Her tears fell on my face as she nodded. "Yes!"

I swung her up into my arms, forgetting all about the ring. I captured her lips and kissed her until neither one of us could breathe. Breaking for air, I whispered, "Thank you for making this real."

"I should be thanking you, Brock. For showing me what real love can be."

Slipping the ring on her finger, I kissed once more, assured by the fact that our picture would be plastered all over social media and the era of the Playboy Player was over.

～

THEA

Two weeks before Spring Training

February was often the coldest month of the year in north Idaho, but I couldn't have cared less. It was our wedding day. The ceremony had been held in a church that had been turned into a full-time wedding venue and it was perfect. The reception took place where our love story began; in the ballroom where I'd bid on and won a date with a bachelor.

"You, Mrs. Cameron, are gorgeous in that dress."

"Why, thank you, Mr. Cameron. Flattery will get you everywhere." I threaded my fingers into my husband's thick mane of dark hair, sighed and pressed my body closer to his as we finished or first dance.

"Oh, I intend to have you...everywhere. I hear the honeymoon suite is very large." Brock wiggled his eyebrows at me. I loved his goofy side. And when it was mingled with his sexy baritone, I was a goner. Not that he'd ever have to beg me to tangle with my favorite player. However, now that we were married, there was something I needed to share.

"How much longer do we need to hang out before we can sneak off to our room?" I grinned at the eagerness in his voice. "You snuck into my bed last night, or rather early this morning. Wasn't that enough to hold you over until later tonight?"

"Define enough?"

"Well...we will need to take any opportunity to have sex, especially with the season beginning next month. Then there's my nausea. I suspect there's going to be days where I won't feel up to it." I held his gaze, trying to keep a straight face.

Brock's lips thinned and his brow narrowed into a V. When the light dawned, and he understood exactly what I was saying without coming right out and saying I was pregnant was glorious. This moment, during a day that I would remember for the rest of my life, will be tucked away and cherished forever.

"When can we tell people?" His hand went to my belly, where his fingers splayed out and cradled my non-existent baby bump. But I couldn't wait until I grew round with our child.

"Let's wait until after the first trimester. I'm so happy, Brock. I can't believe this is my life now. That we found each other and now we're going to have a baby. You have no idea how grateful I am that you didn't give up on me."

Brock pulled me close and kissed my tears. "Oh, sweetheart, don't cry. It's our wedding day."

Laughing, I wound my arms around his neck. "Don't worry. They're happy tears."

∽

Thank you so much for reading this collection. Please consider leaving a review on the retail site you purchased this copy. Reviews help other readers discover books, and it adds to an author's joy meter. – Thank you!

WHAT TO READ NEXT?
ZESTING WITH ZANE

Want to read more stories set in the Pineville world? Click HERE or visit www.debraeliseauthor.com

Want to keep up with Debra's book news? Join her newsletter HERE >>> https://bit.ly/DebraEliseNewsletter

ALSO BY DEBRA ELISE

TANGLING series:

TANGLING WITH MY EX – **Read for free by signing up for my newsletter** HERE,
TANGLING WITH THE BREWMASTER – **Luke + Laci**
TANGLING WITH THE COWBOY - **Lawson + Jana**
WORTH THE WAIT – **Cole + Scarlett**
TANGLING WITH THE PLAYER – **Brock + Thea**
ZESTING WITH ZANE – **Zane + Holly**
RESUCED BY AN OUTLAW – **Dean + Nori**
TANGLING WITH THE MOUNTAIN MAN - **Beck + Taya**
TANGLING WITH THE SILVER FOX **Hayden + Brenley**
MY CUPID HOLIDATE – **Rex + Heather**
TANGLING WITH THE DOCTOR - **Jack + Kiersten**
TANGLING WITH SANTA – **Slade + Kara**
FOR THE LOVE OF CURVES – **Roman + Miranda**
TANGLING WITH THE GRINCH – **Walker + Mazie**
BIDDING ON A COWBOY – **Sawyer + Emma**
CEMENTING HER LOVE – **Colton + Shayla**

COMING IN 2025

GRUMP OF MISTY MOUNTAIN – April 7th
SWEATER LATE THAN NEVER - October 22nd

NEW SERIES:

MOUNTAIN MEN OF PINEVILLE

MOUNTAIN MAN SAVIOR – April 23rd
MOUNTAIN MAN PROTECTOR – May 7th
MOUNTAIN MAN DEFENDER – June 4th

<u>Other Series by Debra Elise:</u>
RESCUED BY LOVE: LATER IN LIFE

LOVE AT EVERMORE & 39TH – **Evan + Cassidy**
LOVE AT SECOND & 49TH – **Kade + Patrice**
LOVE AT FIRST & 35TH – **Sam + Evie**
LOVING GOLDIE – **Ford + Goldie**
LOVE AT FOREVER & 56TH – **Adam + Lois**

RESCUED BY LOVE, also set in the Pineville World, features connected characters tied to the Idaho Outlaws, a professional baseball team and their family and friends.

SAVING MAVERICK – **Maverick + Kelsey**
MANAGING BLAKE – **Blake + Caris**
CHASING NOEL – **TS & Noel**
REDEEMING SCROOGE – **Grant + Sophie**
RESCUING ROYCE – **Royce + Amber**
TEMPTING ZAK – **Zak + Harlowe**

Paranormal Books:

Gods, Monsters, And Magic: (The Brethren's Legacy World)

(third person pov)

Series Page >>> https://geni.us/GodsMonstersandMagic

DRAGON'S GODDESS

WOLF'S MATE

MATED TO THE MONSTER SERIES - Multi-author collaboration (THE BRETHREN'S LEGACY WORLD) Connected characters to those found in the Gods, Monsters, and Magic series. These books can be read as stand alones, but readers are encouraged to read in order beginning with Dragon's Goddess.

(first person pov)

FATED TO THE PHOENIX

FATED TO THE GRIZZLY

FATED TO THE PANTHER

ABOUT THE AUTHOR

Debra Elise, a *USA Today* Bestselling Author, writes steamy contemporary and paranormal romance. She lives with her younger trophy husband and their needy golden doodle, Zander, in the beautiful Pacific Northwest. They also have two young adult sons who have promised to never read her stories.

A self-proclaimed extroverted introvert, when not writing or procrastinating, she enjoys a strong cup of coffee, and a good nap.

www.debraeliseauthor.com

Made in United States
North Haven, CT
22 March 2025